HURT BUT NOT HARMED

STACY ADAMS

HURT BUT NOT HARMED
Stacy Adams

Chicago, Illinois
stacyadams346@gmail.com

©2020 Stacy Adams
ISBN 978-1-949027-67-9

Published by
DestinedToPublish.com | Chicago, Illinois

For my
Granny.

Cornelia Adams

ACKNOWLEDGMENTS

Writing this, my first novel, has been a long but rewarding journey. I have learned so much about myself along the way, and have learned to believe in myself more than I believe in my critics. I'm grateful for the gift of words and for family and friends who were patient enough—for years—to listen to me talk about my dream of becoming an author.

Thank you to my Granny, Cornelia Adams. Your life inspires me to write. Thank you to my parents, Marcia and Michael Jones, and Stephen Wilson Sr. for teaching me to love beyond boundaries. Thank you to my little sister Le-sa for keeping me grounded; five-tre' for life!

Thank you to all those who have passed on but have left an everlasting imprint on my heart. I miss you, Baby Brother. Also, thank you to my extended families: Adams, Jones, Logan, Moore, Wilson, and Valley Kingdom Ministries International.

I couldn't have made it here without you all. To God be the glory for the things He has done.

PREFACE

Is there a difference between hurt and harm? Or is inflicted pain, whether intentional or not, such a marker on the human heart that there's no distinction between the two? Set in 1973, toward the end of the Vietnam War, *Hurt but Not Harmed* looks at the traditional yet changing values of a model black family, post-Civil Rights movement, and the woven secrets they hold as a means of coping or an attempt to thrive.

The Boyds, like many black families, built their family culture on a foundation of love, faith, and resilience. Yet they were challenged with how to use those foundational pillars to the benefit of all. Centering on the story of their vocal matriarch, Ruthie Boyd, *Hurt but Not Harmed* explores the hidden power of silence in a family dynamic and its impact on family lineage if left unaddressed. Ruthie's home is filled with people, each on a journey to discover their own truths and hopefully find their way back to love.

CONTENTS

INTRODUCTION

There were seven people living in a three-bedroom house. Space was limited, but in her eyes, they were still blessed. Ruthie Boyd, the home's matriarch, always said they were well off, but the truth was they were just getting by. She called the Boyds blessed, though, because some folks had no home at all or were forced to cram into one of those so-called high-rises. In her opinion, the only things that rose high in those buildings were green dollars for white builders and false hopes for coloreds.

It was 1973, and Ruthie still called her people *colored.* That was how she was raised, and it was all she knew. She was that way about a lot of things. There was no use changing things if they worked for you, she thought. To her, being colored wasn't a sign of shame, but a medal of honor.

It was summertime. Ruthie and Yvonne spent hours sitting on the front porch. Ruthie talking about the good ole days and Yvonne watching people stroll up the crackled sidewalk along their street. It wasn't the Gold Coast, but for a South Side Chicago neighborhood, they were doing good with thriving trees, green grass, and a sense of community.

There was a local grocery store, a bus stop, and a candy store for the kids—all within walking distance at best. Cars seemed to glide, almost reminiscing about an era gone by. People were still friendly, as if the generation since the Great Migration meant nothing to their way of life. The ones who did act more like city folk at least knew to mind themselves a bit. Yet there was a pulse, a heartbeat of something more brewing beneath the surface, as if what *was* just wasn't enough for people anymore. As if more would be better, at any cost.

Things changed a lot for the Boyd family that summer, especially since people like Yvonne's Daddy were back home from Vietnam. Jimmy was having flashbacks, and nothing seemed to break them until he started hanging out at Joe's Tavern near the candy store. Yvonne started seeing him go in sometimes when she went to buy a Slo Poke after school.

At first Jimmy would say, "Yvonne, baby, Daddy's just having an afternoon beer with the guys." She later found out from Joe's youngest daughter that Jimmy wasn't sitting at the bar at all, but in the back room hiding his sorrows in a white cloud.

This was also the summer Yvonne and Cheryl moved in with Ruthie, the night of the big storm.

Chapter One

SASSAFRAS

"Yvonne. Yvonne! Come help me split these peas," Ruthie called out from the kitchen. "We've got to get things ready for Sunday dinner and I still need you to get to the front room."

"Get to the front room to do what?"

"To clean it, girl! You know what I mean. I don't have time for that sassafras mouth of yours today. Forget the front room for now. Just come in the kitchen here and help me with these peas."

Yvonne always gave her Granny lip about helping prepare for Sunday dinner, but truthfully it was one of her favorite Saturday chores. It always meant Sunday was just one day away. On Sunday she could see her church friends who lived on the other side of King Drive, and maybe even her daddy if Cheryl thought he was clearheaded enough to come for a visit.

"I'm coming, Granny. I just have to wash my hands."

"You're right about that. You 'bout need to wash more than that. You've been out playing Penny with those mannish boys for two hours."

"It's not Penny, Granny. It's Piggy."

"Piggy, Penny, whoever it was, just hurry up. We've got a lot to do, and I don't know where your mother and Aunt Sheila are yet."

"Mama ran out to the store an hour ago, and Auntie Shay, well, she's probably off with her new boyfriend."

"Girl, if you don't watch your mouth. Who do you think you're talking to, one of your little schoolmates?"

"No, Granny, you just asked a question and I answered it."

"Just get in this kitchen, girl."

Although Ruthie had dismissed Yvonne's last remark, her face told a different story. Sheila had been spending a lot of time out lately but said she was taking a few summer classes at the university. She had a full scholarship and kept good grades, there was no doubt about that. Ruthie just wanted to make sure things stayed that way, especially since she hadn't been able to do that for Cheryl, let alone for herself.

Ruthie had lived more than fifty years by the time her youngest child, Sheila, turned eighteen years old. Sheila was definitely an unexpected child, but was loved just as much as her brother and sister. Ruthie was wise, seasoned, and had an answer for almost any problem. Sheila, though, was one of those who had to learn her lessons by jumping straight out of the frying pan and into the fire.

The sound of keys clinked at the door.

"Morning, Mother," Sheila said, entering as if her latest birthday had finally put them on the same level.

"Mother? You should watch how you say that. You might make me think you mean to put another name on the end of that besides Boyd. So what's got you out of the house so early on a Saturday morning?"

"It's twelve o'clock, Mama."

"Yeah, but you've been out of the house since seven."

"I had business to tend to, that's all. How are you, Yvonne?" Sheila asked, changing the subject.

"Fine, Auntie Sheila."

Sheila was always Yvonne's favorite person in the house, besides Ruthie and her mother, of course. Sheila was special, though. Nature and nurture determine how close you are to a mother or grandmother, but common likes and dislikes determine how close you are to a friend. Sheila was Yvonne's friend in the house, partly because they were the closest in age. But outside of that, Yvonne admired Sheila's spunk and sense of class. Some of Yvonne's flippant attitude came from her attempts to emulate Sheila. The rest of it was just plain out Yvonne.

"Auntie Sheila, how's Bobby?"

"Girl, hush up. Whose side are you on here?" Sheila whispered.

"Oops."

Just then Cheryl came in through the back door with a paper bag of groceries tucked underneath each arm. She stopped briefly to speak to Papa Boyd, who was staring vacantly at cowboy flicks on an old black-and-white. She then entered the kitchen with the others.

"Hey, y'all," Cheryl said.

"Good. Someone else is here to take the heat off of my back," Sheila mumbled.

"What heat am I taking off? I might not want it, girl."

"Oh, nothing."

"So, did you recover from your night out with *Bobby*?" Cheryl teased.

"Thanks a lot, Sis. Besides, his real name is Robert—Robert Johnston, thank you very much. It wasn't just the two of us. You make it sound like I was doing something wrong."

"Wrong? Did I say anything about doing anything wrong?"

"Well, I'm about to say it," Ruthie interrupts. "Who is Robert

Johnston? What kind of family name is that, anyway, and why haven't I heard anything about him 'til now? You got something to hide, child?"

"No, Mother Dear." She exaggerated that last word. "Why do you have to make a fuss about every little thing?"

"I don't consider my youngest child's good name a little thing."

"What do you mean by that?" Sheila asked.

"What I mean is, were you really out tending business since 7:00 a.m., or were you just sneaking in from last night?"

"I resent that. I really resent that! How can you say that to me? Have you ever known me to do anything that disrespected your house, let alone you?"

"Hold up, you two, before this thing gets ugly," Cheryl interrupted, now unloading groceries. "I'm sorry I started all of this. I was really only teasing Baby Sis. Anyway, Mama, you know Shay is probably the only eighteen-year-old virgin on earth."

"Thanks a lot, Cheryl. You really know how to lighten a mood. Besides, the name's Sheila, not Shay."

It irked Sheila terribly when Cheryl and her mother used questions to make sly accusations. She hated it even more that people still called her by the nickname she earned the year she lost her two front teeth and had trouble saying her own name. She was an adult now, fully grown, and old enough to be treated with the same level of respect she used to give the "big people" in the family. In her mind, it was age that finally brought respect, not wisdom. The way Sheila saw it, turning eighteen instantly made her a woman.

"Look, Mama, I came in last night at the time you said for me to come in, so that should be the end of it. I don't need this stress right now. My new boss starts today and I want to make a good impression. Maybe I can get that promotion to head clerk. Mr.

Clark says I'm the best worker on the floor. So if I'm lucky, they'll promote me or even move me from lingerie to the perfume counter, where I can get commission sales, too."

"Is that the height of your expectations, Shay?" Ruthie asked.

"What do you mean, Mama?"

"Just what I said. Is that all you're shooting for in life, to be the head clerk in some department store?"

"Why do you always have to down everything I do? Why do you have to question me and act like I can't make my own decisions?"

"I'm not downing you, Shay. I'm just calling it like I see it. I want to make sure you don't lose focus on school, settle, and end up like . . . It's just that you're so young, and—"

"End up like who Mama? Me?" Cheryl asked. "Go on and say it. Or, better yet, I'll say it. She doesn't want you to end up like me." She slammed the canned goods from the now torn paper bag onto the yellow laminate countertop.

"I didn't mean that. Stop. Stop putting words in my mouth! Both of you!"

Suddenly silence entered the room to squelch the growing tension. The only sound was the rhythmic opening and closing of cabinet doors.

It was true; Ruthie really didn't want Sheila to end up like Cheryl. It was Cheryl who gave up a four-year academic scholarship to marry a man who promised the world, but forgot to say it only went as far as Forty-Ninth Street. Ruthie wanted to remind Sheila that the department store was just a stepping stone and that earning her college degree should be the priority. Ultimately, though, what Ruthie really wanted was for Sheila not to end up like her.

Sheila grabbed a handful of pea pods from the large green bowl on the table. She joined Yvonne, who hadn't stopped her steady motions to the bowl since the big people started to shout.

A while later there was a knock at the door.

"I'll get it, Mama," Sheila said sullenly.

"Who is it, Shay?" Ruthie asked. "Shay?"

After getting no response, Ruthie wiped her hands on her flowered apron and walked slowly toward the front room to see for herself. She was just in time to see Sheila and Robert Johnston kiss in the doorway. To prevent any more straining words that early in the day, Ruthie turned back to the kitchen.

"I'm gone, Mama. Robert's gonna give me a lift to the bus stop," Sheila shouted from the front door.

"To the stop," Ruthie whispered to herself. "Why can't he just drive her to work?"

Ruthie had always told her girls that the way you start a relationship is the way it will end up. When she and Papa Boyd were courting, he always made sure he had access to a car to take her to Ms. Pittman's for day work—all the way there.

Things had changed a lot since then. Papa Boyd couldn't move around the house much anymore, let alone drive Ruthie anywhere. Yet she still wanted her girls to taste life's best, even if it didn't last forever.

Ruthie and Yvonne started rinsing and seasoning peas while Cheryl finished unpacking groceries in silence. Each of them hoped that the absence of new words would somehow erase the old. Boyd women were known for speaking their minds. Yet that very similarity made them collide. Each of them really saw the world the same way the others did at that age. It was just that with experience came wisdom and a sense of being less green.

At times they saw the world through the other person's eyes—a clearer set of lenses—yet forgot far too soon what they had just seen. Love in the Boyd household was blind that way. They were often guilty of not only overlooking the bad, but also forgetting to clean the fogged lenses that allowed the bad to happen in the first place.

No more words were spoken, and Cheryl exited the kitchen in favor of the solitude of her bedroom on the second floor.

Slowly the kitchen began to take on the truest sentiment of the woman of the house. Although Ruthie seldom held her tongue, she never wanted to disturb the peace. She never intended to hurt anyone with her words. She only wanted to convey the depth of her love. Sometimes, though, she loved so deeply that people did get hurt. Other times, she loved so deeply because people had been hurt. Her words sometimes contradicted her love, as words often do.

The mood in the whole house gradually became quiet, almost holy. There was always a quiet presence in the Boyd house on Saturday afternoons. It was as if the bricks and mortar themselves knew a holy day was approaching. As if the walls and ceilings opened up to breathe in new life and a fresh start for the week ahead. The pot of boiling peas whistled out steam, an AM gospel station played softly in the background, and for a while, peace rested at the door.

Chapter Two

THE NIGHT

The rest of Saturday passed by quietly. A sun shower watered the lawn and gave brief relief from the hot June sun. By evening, the Boyd house was clean; a maple glazed ham, fresh peas, and all the trimmings were prepared; and Ruthie's famous chocolate-chocolate cake was baking in the oven.

Ruthie and Yvonne spent a couple hours each night sitting in the cedar rockers on the front porch of their family home—1047 Lexington Lane. The house, a two-story white Victorian with a wraparound lattice-trimmed porch, meant the world to the Boyd family. There was a modest front yard with a budding yellow rosebush Ruthie had planted herself. A row of red-green tomatoes and collard greens was planted out back. The house had likely once been the talk of the neighborhood—probably some twenty years before, when whites still lived there with their white picket fences, obedient house dogs, and proper-acting kids.

Things had changed. Whites ran off and blacks moved in. Times had changed. Although most people took pride in their homes, most were housing more people than their homes were made to hold, and the wear and tear of it all was beginning to show. Times of war had a way of forcing people to consolidate their lives. Vietnam sure did.

Some things remained the same, though. The porch talks had become a summer night ritual for Ruthie and her only grandchild. First the two would head straight for the kitchen, Yvonne to the apple-green cabinets for two mason jars, and Ruthie to the fridge for the fresh-made lemonade.

Then, like clockwork, Papa Boyd would awake from his dozing on the enclosed back porch long enough to say, "Who's there?"

Ruthie's response was always the same: "Who do you think?"

That was about the height of their exchange each day, and precisely the problem. Papa Boyd didn't seem to do much thinking anymore, or at least not much talking. Maybe he just had everyone in the house fooled into believing that he didn't do much thinking. Maybe that was all he did, and perhaps he had become a prisoner of his own thoughts.

That was beside the point for Ruthie, though. Right now, she needed a piece of life for herself, and any peace in life itself. Ruthie and Yvonne would scurry out the kitchen and pass the prison of Papa Boyd's thoughts to their nightly escape just beyond the front door.

Now, sitting on the front porch, listening to crickets chirping and a single car coasting down the one-way lane, each creak of the cedar rocking chairs moved Ruthie closer to her goal.

"Granny? What do you suppose people do in their homes at night?" Yvonne asked. "I can see the lights on through their closed drapes, so I know they're still awake. What do you think they may be doing in there, all cooped up like chickens?"

"Not everyone enjoys sitting out on the porch, taking in the night air like you and I do, Yvonne. We're like night owls. We can do some of our best thinking at night. Other people would rather ignore the night like it's not even there." Ruthie paused for a sip of lemonade. "But people like you and me—we embrace the light and the dark just the same. We take the good with the bad and still manage to be all right. For us, it doesn't matter if it's eighty-five degrees with a cool lake breeze or whether there's a thunderstorm that came out of nowhere. Sometimes the best lessons in life come out of the storms you never saw coming. People like you and me are okay with that."

"Well, I just think they stay cooped up because they're scared. They don't want to be around people who hang out on the streets at night. Even though we don't see a lot of people doing wrong, we know they're still doing it. I think the people inside the houses are really just scared to come out, even if it is just out on the front porch. That's what I think."

"You have a good point there. That makes a lot of sense, too. People fear the dark like they fear death. Both have gotten a bad rap through the years. Think about it: death and taxes. Till death do us part. Death holds a pretty strong commitment that most people just don't want to make. And when they do, it's usually over their dead body!"

"Granny, you're funny," Yvonne chuckled. "Does Papa Boyd know how funny you are, Granny? I think he might talk to you more if he knew you were funny."

"Your Papa Boyd knows a lot of stuff about me. Sometimes I think I told him too much along the way. I think maybe I put his brain in overdrive with some of the things I've said these thirty years, and his mind just wasn't able to drive that fast. I think he finally got into neutral and just stayed there. Heck, who am I fooling? He's in park!"

The pair slowly sipped their lemonades, rocking in a syncopated rhythm. They spent the next hour in a conversation of hearts even though few words were spoken. Ruthie and Yvonne's connection flowed together like the unsung harmony to a song—those who hear music know it's there even when the notes aren't played. Mirror images. Then and now. Before and after. So there they sat, looking up at the stars: one planning her future among the "big," the other reminiscing about the big things that could have been.

"Well, enough about that. I think it's time we turn in for the night ourselves. We've got a busy day tomorrow and I don't want you fussing with your Mama about getting up in time to go to Sunday School."

"Why do I have to go to Sunday School, anyway? They teach the same stuff year after year, and besides, I've got you to ask if I have a question."

"Girl, you need all the Bible learning you can get. It'll come in handy someday. Now hand me those empty mason jars down there on the floor. While you're at it, give me a lift out of this chair."

"Tell me the story about these rocking chairs again, Granny. How Ms. Pittman willed them to you, and how it took her son a year and a half to track you down because you moved from down South."

"I think you just did."

"Oh, Granny, you're just saying that because you want me to go in the house."

"I'm guilty as charged. Now, let's go."

Inside, Cheryl is watching the late-night news, and Sheila, back from work, is thumbing through the latest issue of *Jet Magazine*.

"Cheryl, did you know that Los Angeles just elected a black mayor?"

"No, I didn't know. Who?"

"It says right here that Thomas Bradley is their new mayor-elect."

"Wouldn't it be nice if Chicago had a colored mayor, too?" Ruthie added, stepping into her house shoes and walking over to her plastic slip-covered white wingback chair.

"We're *black*, Mama. Why do you insist on calling us that?" Sheila asked.

"Yeah, Mama. James Brown says, 'I'm black and I'm proud,'" Cheryl said with a chuckle. "Aren't you proud to be black?"

"*Colored* is powerful enough to me. When I was a girl, we

looked forward to being called anything other than out of our name, and when it finally happened, we embraced it. After all, the organization is called the NAACP, right? Never mind that some folks later put a bad light on colored, too. We had already taken it on as a badge of honor. I still do."

Ruthie took any opportunity to talk about how colored folk once had some of the best neighborhoods around. Atlanta had Auburn; New York had its Harlem Renaissance; and her Sweet Home Chicago had Bronzeville. She often bragged about how she watched Chicago fill up with coloreds seeking a better chance in life through steady pay at the steel mills, stockyards, and railroads. Ruthie often reminisced about how colored communities were filled with their own doctors, lawyers, schools, restaurants, stores, insurance companies and even banks. She reminisced as if the best of her and her people was rooted in an era gone by.

"We had our own because we had to; we worked hard because we needed to; and we respected each other's things because we knew ourselves how hard it was to get them.

"Money was hard to come by back when we got this house. Heck, it still is. But back then coloreds had few choices and little chance of making it on their own. So we stuck together. In kitchenettes, in two-bedroom apartments, sleeping four and five to a bed, we stuck together. We lived together, worked together, struggled together.

"At 1047 Lexington Lane, we did the same. What made us different on the inside was how we saw the world on the outside. I always quoted the Bible character Joshua: 'As for me and my house—"

"We will serve the Lord," Cheryl and Sheila chimed in and chuckled in unison.

"Hey, what can I say?" Ruthie added. "I know I'm on my soapbox, but that's why we've been here all this time. We *knew* who to give thanks to!"

"Well, amen, Reverend Ruthie," Cheryl mocked. "Sounds like

you're getting a practice run for your first sermon. Are you up to bat tomorrow morning?"

"Amen," Sheila laughed. "Yeah, I can grab an empty box of Borax for her to stand on if you'd like."

"Well since the dynamic duo wants to try to signify and shut me down, how was work today, Shay?" Ruthie asked.

"I wasn't trying to shut you down, Mama. That was Cheryl."

"I beg your pardon, Ms. Anne. You were right there with me with your amens, too," Cheryl rebutted.

"Anyway, Mama, work was just fine. They started training me on how to count down all the drawers in my department today. I think the next step will be a key to the lockbox."

"Man, you're pretty highfalutin' down there at Montgomery Ward, then," Cheryl said.

"I don't know about all of that, but I will say that folks respect me there. New workers are always coming to me with their questions. And the old workers trust me to watch their backs. It may not be all that to some people, but it means a lot to me."

Ruthie took her glasses out of her apron pocket and slowly placed them on the tip of her nose. No, she may not have had twenty-twenty vision anymore, but she could surely read between the lines. It was clear who "some people" were to Sheila, but instead of making a comment, Ruthie just tapped her foot to an internal countdown while reaching for the early edition of the Sunday *Sun-Times*.

"Well, good for you, little sis," Cheryl said.

"Okay, Mama, I'm going to bed," Yvonne interrupted, back from washing the mason jars in the kitchen sink.

"No, Missy. I don't think so," Cheryl said. "You smell like a little nanny goat. You need to get your behind in that bathtub. You should know that if you don't take a bath any other night of the week, it sure better be Saturday night. And go bring me the comb and brush and the Queen Bergamot too, so I can do your hair."

"Cheryl, that girl's almost a teenager," Sheila interrupted. "It's about time you let her put a comb to her own head. That's embarrassing."

"I'm the mama here, thank you very much."

"Mama, what's the big deal about Saturday night baths anyway?" Yvonne questioned, as if the weight of her words was equal to the big people she tried to avoid. She had already retrieved the comb and brush from the bathroom sink and took a seat between Cheryl's feet. Cheryl combed through Yvonne's twisted ponytails to re-braid them.

"The big deal is that on Sunday morning, you're going to church to see the King of Kings and Lord of Lords, and you don't present yourself before royalty dirty," Ruthie interjected, glancing up from the front page. "You can't stand before a king looking any ole kind of way.

"Plus, when I was growing up down South, fresh water was a high commodity. We didn't have indoor plumbing and you didn't just go around drawing well water for every little thing, especially not in a house with a mother, father, twelve kids, and cattle to feed. So, Saturday night was when we made the sacrifice and filled the steel tub with well water that Mama heated up on the coal stove. And all of us children took turns bathing in that same tub of water."

"You mean the same tub filled with fresh water for each child, right?" Yvonne asked.

"Now didn't I tell you fresh water was a high commodity? Of course we didn't each get fresh water. Mama would keep dunking us in the water until it just got too dirty and then, and only then would she send one of us out to the well for some more.

"There was a lot of sharing going on. We shared water, clothes, shoes, and even our beds. My Mama had seven boys and five girls, and I was the fourth-born girl. By the time I got an outfit, it had already been worn by three of my sisters. I always got hand-me-downs, never new clothes. And us three youngest girls shared a double bed together for as long as I can remember.

"So you have a lot to be grateful for, young lady. I wish I could have had a bath all to myself inside a house with warm running water when I was your age. Heck, you even have a choice of two tubs. If I were you, I'd waltz up those stairs to the bathroom like I was Queen of the Nile, draw my bathwater, and lavish in every second of it."

"Wow. I never knew that, Granny. Why didn't you tell me that story before?"

"I've got a-plenty more I haven't told you, too, but for now go take your bath."

"Okay, Granny."

Yvonne retrieved the comb and brush from Cheryl, who had just finished her new braids, and obediently went up the creaky wooden staircase to the second floor.

"Mama," Cheryl said, "I just don't get it. I can tell that child to do something ten times and she'll argue with me every single time. You chime in and mention something once, and it's done. Just like that, no questions asked. Why is that?"

"Cheryl, that's no ill reflection on you. Yvonne and I have an understanding that even we don't fully understand. It's just the way it is, I guess. I reason with her. I don't compromise, but I do reason. She's as smart as a whip and she's focused like an arrow. She just needs to know what direction you're pointing her in before she'll fly."

"Hmm. Don't we all," Cheryl said. "Don't we all."

SERVICE

Jesus is on the main line, tell him what you want.
Oh, Jesus is on the main line, tell him what you want.
The line is never busy, tell him what you want.
The line is never busy, tell him what you want.
Tell him, tell him, tell him what you want.
You just call him up and tell him what you want.

•

"I wish it were that easy," Cheryl thought to herself.

There she was in Bethesda Baptist Church, singing the words to a song she didn't believe. Cheryl had prayed and cried out to God so many times, until she felt He must be tired of listening. Three years of praying and crying, and still no results. Her prayer was simple. "Lord, bring my husband Jimmy home with every limb intact." Sure, Jimmy returned to Chicago with every limb intact and all ten toes, all ten fingers. Only thing missing was his soul. Jimmy the person came back, but his personality was lost somewhere in the jungles of Vietnam.

The Jimmy who volunteered for the army to bring home a steady paycheck to his family was vibrant and alive. He stood six-foot-two with dark brown eyes and a tailored Afro. He loved music, played the trumpet in a local jazz band, and even had dreams of recording an album. Cheryl had come to think maybe she should have been more supportive of his dream rather than complaining of not having enough from his sporadic gigs to keep a roof over their heads. Maybe if she'd gotten a better job or went back to school to help out, he never would have felt the need to volunteer for war in the first place. He had already been skipped for the draft. Maybe if they hadn't bought that Olds Cutlass, there would have been extra money in the account. Maybe if they hadn't gotten married so young and hadn't been struggling to raise Yvonne. Maybe—

"Thank ya! Thank ya! Thank you, Jesus!" A woman's shouts for joy from the next pew broke into Cheryl's thoughts of despair.

"Boy, I tell you," Cheryl murmured to herself. "You can't even find peace with your thoughts in the house of God."

The congregation's overture of shouts of joy and release succumbed to the humming wails and melodious chords of the Hammond B-3 organ. With music now softly playing in the background, the pastor, garbed in his black robe with crimson trim, mounted the pulpit.

"Brothers and sisters, today's message comes from the story of Job and is one that I've toiled with for the past three days. It's not an easy word, but it's a right word," the Reverend Benjamin Falls began. "Today's sermon title is 'Secrets of the Night.'

"Brothers and sisters, think back to when you were a child. How many of you were afraid of the dark? Come on, now. Be honest. I'll admit it—the dark was a scary place. Especially out there in the country, where I grew up; at nightfall, you couldn't even see your hand in front of your face. Once my mama cut off the kerosene lamp, that was it. Forget about any monsters under the bed—I was worried about how I would make it to the outhouse if I had to go in the middle of the night. What if I crossed paths with a bat or even a snake?"

"Okay, where is he going with this one?" Cheryl mumbled under her breath.

"The night is something else, isn't it? Even now, as adults, we find ourselves afraid of what we can't see, the unknown. It's still the things we can't see that make us nervous.

"That's why faith is so important in our lives. It's the evidence of things not seen, and evidence is proof that something really exists. Faith is like a spiritual version of that teddy bear your mama used to give you to comfort you through the night. Or even that little G.I. Joe action figure you tucked under your pillow for protection. But now some of us don't rely on faith, that spiritual teddy bear, or G.I. Joe, if you will. Some of us think that since we're grown, it's best to rely on good ole common sense to navigate our way through the dark unknown."

"What else is there to rely on?" Cheryl said to herself underneath the building sea of amens.

"Truth be told, we rely on our common sense probably more than anything else. Even more than common sense, some of us rely on our past experiences to find our way through new, unfamiliar territory—through the unseen future. Only problem with that is that some of our past experiences weren't so good. Some of those experiences were downright hurtful. They were like those bats and snakes I was afraid of back there in the country. Like they all just jumped out and attacked you all at once. You know—the hurts that just come at us from out of nowhere.

"Think about it: Like Job learned, the things that hurt us the most are the things we never saw coming. If we saw them ahead of time, we would duck to avoid them. So to hide the embarrassment of being blindsided, we try to keep it a secret that something jumped out at us in the dark. For pride's sake, we don't want anyone to know about how much those bat- and snakelike experiences hurt us, but they hurt us just the same."

Cheryl's prior cynicism gave way to silence. She usually enjoyed Reverend Falls's sermons; she just didn't get this one. Did she wake up on the wrong side of the bed this morning? And what did it have to do with her, anyway? What did it have to do with Jimmy? After all, she'd been praying for three years now and still there was no change. Jimmy was still Jimmy. He volunteered to serve his country. She was in church to serve her God. Yet nothing seemed to work out for either of them. Their service seemed to go unrewarded. There was no medal of honor, no honorable discharge. Where was all the happiness that was supposed to come to people for doing the right thing?

For a moment, Cheryl lost track of the words falling like dew from heaven. She knew they were supposed to refresh her soul, yet they just seemed to sit on the surface of her heart. Instead she gazed over at Yvonne, her woman-child, seated beside her, and then out the stained glass window of a cross that was dedicated to the late Mother Hattie B. Jenkins. Then she slid her fingertips repeatedly over the arm of the oak pew with its nameplate in honor of Brother Willis; rest his soul. She looked at anything, anything to shift her focus until the dewdrops fell even harder.

"Some hurts you just never really get over. Sure, you learn to deal with them and pretend to move on, but it's like shards of an emotional grenade are still lodged in your heart," Reverend Falls continued.

"Hurts like that leave scars on your heart like road maps reminding you where not to go. They are constant reminders of past pains. Some of us are fortunate enough to overlook the painful reminders of the scars. Instead of road maps, we can view those scars as the texture and veins that keep a good heart pumping. Yet the rest of us are so busy trying to save face and hide the shame that true healing can never come."

"Huh? What am I hiding? Everyone in here knows my business," Cheryl muttered.

"Excuse me, Sister. I'm trying to hear the message," a lady in the pew ahead whispered back toward Cheryl.

"Hurt is a powerful tool," Reverend Falls continued. "It brings out either the fear in you or the pride in you. You're tempted to do one or the other, whether you actually do it or not. I'll prove it to you. Just think about a time when your bee-ida sweetie decided to move on for a new and improved model. Hm? Or what about the time you got passed over for that job you really needed to make ends meet. Huh? Or when that jive turkey at the auto shop conned you out of your hard-earned cash money? For some of you, it may have just been the first time you burned your hand on a hot stove. Whatever your hurt was, the reaction was just the same. Either your initial response was to shrink back in fear or to lash out in pride. Very few of us can honestly say we initially overlooked the wrong done to us like it never happened. That's what the Good Book tells us to do, right?

"With the good Lord's help, we may eventually get there, but we don't always start there. The bottom line is that our human nature wants to make sure we never have to experience that hurt, that secret dark place, ever again."

"That's exactly my point," Cheryl said.

"Mama, are you all right?" Yvonne asked.

"Yeah, I'm fine, Yvonne. Just peachy keen."

"Most of us take it a step further, though," Reverend Falls continued. "We keep it a secret as if not ever speaking of the hurt again will make us forget about the pain. Like somehow never mentioning it makes us secretly stronger. But the real secret is that those dark, cold places breed unhealthy things like bitterness and unforgiveness, just like a spiritual mold.

"Brothers and sisters, I challenge you today to shine the light of love on that dark experience. Let the light shine in. Let the real healing begin. Let's not put on the shield of fear or pride to convince ourselves that we're okay. Put on the shield of faith! Put the Word into action! Let the light of God shine into that old, hidden darkness! Clear out the cobwebs of that dark place and get free today!"

The congregation rose to one final tidal wave of hallelujahs and amens as Reverend Falls's sermon came to a close. The sermon's end was met with a resounding chorus of *This Little Light of Mine*, the passing of collection plates, and the hand of fellowship.

Cheryl rose to her feet as though she were on autopilot. What was Reverend Falls saying? Was he implying that it was her own fault that things were going so wrong for her and Jimmy? How could he possibly mean that she was to blame?

The now red-cloaked pastor made his way up the aisle for his weekly meet and greet with the parishioners filing out through the sanctuary's double doors. Cheryl, after a few shallow hugs and half-smiles here and there, made her way farther up the line but momentarily lost the reverend's attention to Mother Martha Jackson, who presented him with one of her famous sweet potato pies.

"Reverend Falls. Reverend Falls!" Cheryl called out.

"Oh, praise the Lord, Sister Cheryl," said Reverend Falls apologetically, turning to greet Cheryl over his shoulder. "How are you this blessed day?"

"Not so good, Reverend Falls."

"Well what seems to be the matter, Sister Cheryl?"

"With all due respect, were you trying to say in your sermon that my life is messed up because I'm spending too much time focusing on the hurts? Pain is real, Reverend Falls. It's really real."

"I wasn't speaking of any one person at all, Sister, but to all of us, myself as well. All of us have been hurt by things and secretly nursed that pain for a little too long. All I'm saying is to give the Lord a chance to really heal our hearts from whatever the hurt may be. You know what I mean—the stuff beneath the surface."

"I hear you, but you just don't understand. I wouldn't be this blunt with you normally. You just struck a nerve, that's all. I—I just don't think you understand."

"Sister Cheryl, I'd love to talk with you longer, but there are more people waiting to be greeted. Please don't take this the wrong way, but hopefully we can pick up this discussion later. My wife and

I have been invited to your mother's for Sunday dinner. Perhaps this would make for a lively discussion then."

"Yes, I guess."

"Mom. Mom!" Yvonne yelled, interrupting Cheryl's train of thought from behind.

"Yes, Yvonne?"

"I'm going outside with my friends."

"I think you mean to say, 'May I go outside with my friends?'"

"Yes. May I?" Yvonne replied curtly.

"Girl! Just go. Go. We'll be leaving right after your Granny has her Willing Workers meeting, so watch out for your Uncle John. He'll be coming to pick us up soon. Tell your Auntie Shay, too."

STICKS AND STONES

Yvonne took her mother's instructions as her cue to round up her friends for a game of hopscotch. She figured if she pulled out the sky blue chalk first, she could avoid the embarrassment of another brutal round of double Dutch. Of all the games she loved to play, double Dutch was never one she perfected. While the other girls had been learning how to jump rope the year of Mrs. Ingle's third grade class, Yvonne had been too busy beating the boys at their own games. They were always teasing the girls about how weak they were. Yvonne felt it her duty to prove them wrong, so she learned to climb trees, run bases, and play Piggy with the best of them. Yet she still longed for that girly thing. She mastered hopscotch because it spoke of having high goals and aspirations even before she was old enough to understand them. Who wouldn't want to reach a place called *sky blue*?

"I brought my pink and blue chalk. Who wants to play?" Yvonne said, taking control of the playground protocol.

Three girls answered Yvonne's call and were soon picking out their own rocks and sketching on the church's rear sidewalk. Blocks one, two, and three were drawn, now onward to ten, and finally, sky blue. The anticipation of yet another conquest was building for Yvonne. Destiny was literally just a hop, skip, and a jump away when the unexpected happened.

"Look at Yvonne and her little flunkies playing in the dirt," teased Tommy Stokes.

Yvonne thought she had finally escaped him and his bullying

23

crew when she moved on to fourth grade and Tommy got left behind. Now, nearly four years later, she was sure to have dodged his direct line of fire. Unfortunately, Tommy's mother decided to find salvation this particular summer at Bethesda Baptist. Of all the churches in the world, she had to pick the one the Boyds had called their spiritual home three generations deep. So now, not only had Yvonne not escaped Tommy Stokes, they were destined to spend eternal life together.

"Hey, you heard me. You, over there playing in the dirt like a little pig."

"I'm not playing in the dirt, and I'm not a little pig," Yvonne cut back. "You're the one with the flunkies wagging behind you."

"Hey, Yvonne. I bet you've got a tail growing out your butt right now."

"I do not!"

"Do too, and I'm gonna prove it!"

Just then Tommy grabbed a stray stick off the ground and proceeded to chase Yvonne like a two-step dance around the magnolia tree. The goal of his game was simple—push up the back of her blue and green plaid printed dress to reveal what he just knew to be her biggest secret. After going a few rounds about the tree and shouting for Tommy to leave her alone, Yvonne had finally had enough and stood flat-footed before him. In one split second, she went from crying out for help to being her own rescue squad. Before she knew it, she had balled up her right fist and punched Tommy Stokes square in the jaw.

"Yvonne! Yvonne! Girl, what are you doing?" Sheila called out from the church walkway and rushed toward her.

"Huh?"

"Huh, nothing! Why did you just hit Tommy?"

"He—he was trying to push up my dress, Auntie Shay! He called

24

me a pig and said he was going to show everyone my tail!"

"Now, Tommy, is that true?"

"I was just playing with her, that's all, Miss Sheila," Tommy whimpered, choking back tears of pain and embarrassment.

"Well, Tommy, you can't play with young ladies that way. And, little Miss Yvonne, that's what I expect you to act like, a young lady. Now, tell each other you're sorry, and Tommy, you go on your way."

"Sorry, Miss Sheila. Sorry, Yvonne."

"I'm sorry, too."

Truth be told, Yvonne was more hurt than Tommy Stokes could ever be. She was humiliated, but just too proud to cry. Somehow, though, she instinctively transformed her fear into the adrenaline she needed to stand her ground. Perhaps she had come to her own understanding of Reverend Falls's Sunday message by confronting a past hurt head-on.

"Yvonne, now say goodbye to your friends." Sheila instructed.

"But we didn't even get a chance to play hopscotch."

"I know you didn't. So consider that your punishment. Or would you rather I tell your Mama or even your Granny?"

"No, Auntie Sheila."

"Well then, don't lollygag. Say goodbye and let's go."

Just then Uncle John pulled up in time to sweep the Boyd family away from the scene of the crime—the crime of injury with a deadly weapon of words against little Tommy's future manhood and Yvonne's feminine pride.

Uncle John grew up in Bethesda, but when Dr. King was assassinated and then three friends died in what he called a senseless war, he didn't see much sense in praying to a God that seemed to ignore such tragedy. Uncle John was Granny's only son. He still lived at home, if rare appearances counted as living there. He could afford his own place; he just didn't want to be alone. He had not yet married or had children, so he worked at the bus depot, spent his spare time at the NAACP, and spent his spare money helping Ruthie and Papa Boyd pay a few bills. As for church, he saw little use in spending two or even three hours singing and shouting about an invisible force when there were visible battles to fight. John was still a good man with a big heart, big enough to drive his family to and from a place they believed to be a place of rest, refuge, and release.

"What's happenin', Yvonne and Shay? Y'all about ready to go?" John asked, making a single motion with his right hand while stepping out of his 1967 silver El Dorado.

"Just about. Mama should be finishing up with the Willing Workers in a little while. They're planning a bake sale. As for me? I've been here policing Miss Yvonne," Sheila said.

"Policing? What Yvonne need policing for now? Do I need to call the pigs for real? Yvonne, what'd you do?"

"Nothing, Uncle John. I was just minding my own business, trying to play hopscotch with my friends, when that snotty-nose Tommy Stokes comes messing with me."

"Messing with you how?"

"He called me a pig and picked up a stick to try to show people I had a tail under my dress."

"He what?"

"Now, John, before you go sending out the militia, just know that Little Miss Yvonne more than handled things herself."

"Oh, really?"

"Yeah, she punched the poor boy in the face."

"Well, good for you. I'm not for hurting our own, but it sounds like he had that one coming."

"John, she doesn't need you condoning that."

"I'm not condoning that, Shay. Didn't I just say I'm not one for hurting our own? The man's got that covered enough for all of us. I'm just saying there are times when a lady has to stand up for herself, and this was one of them."

"That's just it—a lady. A lady doesn't handle herself that way, John. We're trying to teach her how to conduct herself like a lady at all times."

"That's fine and dandy, Shay, but let one of these good ole deacons come up to you, trying to raise your dress in front of all of King Drive, and see how you react."

"So did you give 'em a black eye, Yvonne?"

"No, Uncle John. I missed."

"Hilarious! Oh, my goodness, you are too funny. You remind me of your Mama when she was your age. Her schoolyard bully's name was Randy Jenkins, but he went by Roscoe. Boy, he would tease Cheryl something awful. Roscoe Jenkins. He'd be pulling her ponytail one day, and stepping on her black and white saddle shoes the next. Till one day they had a standoff, too."

"So what did Mama do?"

"She threw a rock at his shin! That boy couldn't run bases for three days!"

"John, why are you telling this girl that story?" Sheila asked. "You're gonna make her think what she did was okay."

"She knows what she did wasn't okay. She's a smart little cookie. I was just sharing a story. Shay, you have to admit this is kind of funny. Does Cheryl know?"

"No, I already punished her. Don't see the need in taking it any further."

"I agree. Yvonne, don't make this a habit though. You hear me?"

"Yes, Uncle John."

"Besides, the little boy only picks on you because he likes you."

"Ugh. Tommy Stokes? No way!"

"Yes way. Trust me. The male species is weird that way. I even did it. Still do to a certain degree. We just get nervous about approaching girls we really like. So we end up doing silly things to get their attention. Stupid things, really."

"Well, I don't believe it! Tommy's always so mean to me. He's always calling me names."

"Yvonne, your uncle is right. The same thing has happened to me. And with Tommy being so young, he doesn't even know what he's feeling, let alone how to express it. So you have to take the high road here. You have to help him know that the right way to approach a lady is not by embarrassing her, but by complimenting her."

"I would only do that if I liked him, and I don't! He's always saying mean things to me and hurting my feelings. I would never like him."

"Never?" Sheila asked coyly.

"Never!"

"Look, guys! Here comes Mama now. Did she cook anything good?" John asked. "Man, there goes Reverend Falls, too. Dang it. I'm getting back in the car."

"There's no sense in dodging him, big brother. He *is* coming over for dinner, you know."

"I'm gonna drive around the block. I'll be back."

No sooner had John's El Dorado sneaked around the corner than Ruthie emerged from the church's double doors with her white pillbox hat, slipping into her white Sunday go-to-meeting gloves as if she had just finished official business for the Lord Himself.

"Cheryl, have you seen your brother John yet?" Ruthie asked. "We need to hurry to the house to warm up dinner before the reverend and first lady come over. I asked your Papa to put those Parker House rolls in the oven at one-thirty, but you know he probably fell asleep in front of the TV again."

"I thought I just saw his car go that way," Cheryl said, looking over her shoulder. "Here come Shay and Yvonne now."

The Boyd women reunited on the steps of the church. John reappeared just in time to get them home to prepare for their turn to entertain church royalty.

* * *

It was Sister Ruthie Boyd's Sunday to host the pastor and his wife for dinner. On the menu were the favorites: candied sweets, fresh green peas, macaroni and cheese, collard greens, hot water cornbread, and her specialty – maple-glazed ham. Ruthie often said that anybody could fry the good old gospel bird, but it took time to bake a ham.

It was considered an honor to host a pastor for dinner. After dinner, all the big people gathered in the front room for coffee, but there was a lot more going on than coffee pouring. Ruthie said that when she was a little girl, Sunday coffee with the pastor was the way her parents kept up with what was happening in the community, like what the NAACP was up to, and how they found out about voting rights and opportunities for work and housing in the North.

Reverend Falls, his wife Ida, and Ruthie were first to the dining room table. Sheila brought down an extra chair from upstairs and Cheryl joined the group reluctantly.

The boarder, Mr. Pratt, came downstairs for dinner, too. Sundays were the only time he really interacted with the entire Boyd family all at once. He was even more of a loner than Papa Boyd, who made a rare guest appearance at the dinner table since there were special guests.

John, usually seeking an opportunity to drill ministers about their work or lack thereof to continue Dr. King's struggle, sat down quietly out of respect for Ruthie and just in time for grace.

"Oh, Sister Boyd, everything looks delicious," Ida Falls said.

"Yes, Sister Boyd, looks like you've outdone yourself yet again," Reverend Falls added.

"Well, we'll all be the judge of that," Ruthie said. "Reverend Falls, would you do the honors?"

After a brief moment for grace by the reverend and the slicing of the ham by Papa, the big people took their rightful places around the dining room table. Papa Boyd and Reverend Falls were seated at either head of the table, and their wives to their rights. Cheryl and John both danced around the chair farthest from the right Reverend as if physical distance would convey their stance. John won the tango. Yvonne and the Falls's daughter JoAnne headed for pre-served plates on the makeshift kiddie table in the kitchen.

"Everybody dig in. I'll start with the macaroni and cheese if you'll pass that down my way, Cheryl," Ruthie said.

"Reverend Falls, that was a wonderful sermon this morning," Ruthie said, sparking a conversation. "Wasn't it, Cheryl? Just absolutely wonderful."

"Sister Boyd, you're all too kind. I'm just a humble servant letting the good Lord use me."

"I'll say. I was just having a talk with my grandbaby about what people do behind closed doors at night, and there you go this morning with 'Secrets of the Night.' Look at God."

"He is amazing, isn't He?" Reverend Falls said.

"Dear, the part I loved the most was when you said that hurts can leave scars on your heart like a road map reminding you where not to go. That's so true. We get shell-shocked sometimes over things that hurt us and we just don't know how to move on," Ida said. "Please pass the peas."

"Shell-shocked? The boys back from Vietnam are the ones who can say something about being shell-shocked," John chimed in. "How do you just move on from that?"

"Brother John, I don't believe my wife was making light of anything related to the brutality of war. Were you, dear?"

"No, I wasn't. Not at all."

"What I was saying," interjected Reverend Falls, "is that sometimes we hold on to our pride as protection to shield our hearts from feeling any more pain. And as a result, we often miss out on the real healing that God wants for our lives."

"Reverend Falls, I hear you, but I still don't agree," Cheryl said. "Some hurts are so painful that you're doing good just to pick up the pieces of your life. I don't think that's being too prideful. I think that's just common sense. God gave us a brain. Seems He'd be pleased by us using it, wouldn't He?"

"Now, Cheryl, that's a bit much," Ruthie said, trying to recant her daughter's last statement.

"It's perfectly all right, Sister Boyd," Reverend Falls said. "Cheryl can speak her mind about my sermon. I welcome the feedback.

"Cheryl, yes, God gave us a mind and I believe He wants us to use common sense. But I also think He wants us to use our common sense through the perspective of His word. We have to take on the mind of Christ. Our mind says, 'You hurt me, so I'm gonna hurt you back.' But Christ's mind says, 'You hurt me, and I'll love you anyway.'"

"I don't see what love has to do with any of it. If someone has hurt you, they obviously don't love you. So love is no longer in the equation," Cheryl said. "Butter, please."

"I'm with you on that one, Sis," John interjected.

"And besides, even if I still have love in my heart toward a person, it doesn't mean feeling that way works to my benefit," Cheryl added. "I've gotten hurt a-plenty doing things and accepting things that I really shouldn't have just because I loved someone. And what did that get me? Don't I have to love myself, too? Heck, I should love myself first! After all, the Good Book does say 'Love thy neighbor as thyself.' How can I love my neighbor as I love myself if I don't first love myself?"

"Cheryl, what's gotten into you today?" Ruthie lamented. "I'm sorry, Reverend Falls. I guess you just struck a bad nerve."

"Cheryl, the Bible says, 'He who is without sin, let him cast the first stone,'" Reverend Falls said. "I know you're hurting. And from the little bit that I know of your situation, you have every right to be hurt. But I have to challenge you—drop your stones, Cheryl. Don't throw them.

"My sweet wife here is mild-natured, but don't let that fool you. She's one of the toughest people I've ever met. I put her through some horrible things a few years back that I'm not proud of at all. I won't go into all the details right now, but somehow she found it in her heart to forgive me. So I know firsthand that God can heal a hurting heart. We just have to let Him."

"Mrs. Falls, what did Reverend Falls do bad enough to get *you* rattled?" Cheryl egged her on sarcastically. "I mean, really. He's a man of the cloth, right? What, did he forget to take out the trash one night or leave your favorite dress at the dry cleaners? Did he forget to pay Ma Bell on time or take a twenty-dollar bill from the collection plate? Oh, I know, huh? He must have cheated!"

Suddenly there was an awkward silence in the room. A silence the Boyd house knew all too well. Once again, one of the Boyd women had spoken their mind beyond the limits of return. This time, though, the words pulled back the layers of an outsider's bed of ease.

Cheryl knew her last statement about Reverend Falls had been over the top. She'd flat-out accused him of cheating on his wife right in front of the woman and the entire family during a sacred Sunday dinner. In between "Pass the peas" and "May I have some cornbread?" came her tongue lashes toward a man barely her equal.

Why was she challenging him so? Was she really questioning his integrity as a man of the cloth? Did today's sermon really strike a sour chord that hard? Or was she merely feeling the final blow that broke the dam holding back her own flood of pain?

Cheryl and Jimmy argued that way all the time. She could never seem to let up. It was never enough to have the final say. She always felt uncontrollably compelled to win, to inexplicably push the issue no matter what the issue was. Her internal motto seemed to be, "Don't stop 'til you see the red in their eyes." But this time, there was nothing fair in love and war.

Papa Boyd, Sheila, and Mr. Pratt broke the silence only with the clanging, syncopated fork motions they had focused on all the while. They each saw early on that the waters of this conversation were too murky for their tongues. Then there was Ruthie, whose embarrassment for her daughter and now her pastor left her miraculously speechless. John inwardly gloated over what now seemed his proven concept, that religion was a farce to divert the focus of his people. So there was Cheryl, emotionally all alone in the room. Her words were in the air already and there was no way to retrieve them. Only thing to do now was to hope that somehow new words could fill in the blank pieces of this puzzling conversation.

"Well, I guess you finally found me out," Reverend Falls humbly admitted.

"Reverend Falls, I—I'm . . . I'm so sorry," Cheryl said. "And

Mrs. Falls, I never knew any of this. I'm—I'm . . . You've just always been such a quiet woman. You never complained. I never heard any buzz at church. You're not even saying anything right now.

"I—I don't mean to get in your business, but what was going through your mind? I don't know what happened, but why did you stay? How could you stay?"

"Cheryl, have you lost your mind?" Ruthie interrupted. "This has gone too far! This is not fit dinner conversation and certainly not with the pastor's wife. How dare you?"

"No, Sister Boyd. It's perfectly fine." Ida spoke just above a whisper.

"Honey, this isn't necessary," Reverend Falls insisted. "You don't owe any explanations. If anything, I'm the one who owes something—an apology."

"Sweetheart, you've done all the apologizing necessary, and to the ones who matter the most in this matter—me and God. Cheryl needs to know. She needs to understand. Old wounds show people that healing can happen. So let me show her my wounds.

"The best way I can explain it, Cheryl, is that this last bout of spiritual tests left me bruised but not beaten, hurt but not harmed. I'm not saying that Reverend Falls didn't hurt me. He did, and he did a good job of it. I'm not saying that it was easy to forgive. As a matter of fact, I hated him for a long time. But somehow, Cheryl, I was able to tap into a strength that was bigger than mine. I didn't have the strength to forgive him. I didn't want to forgive him, yet somehow I had no other choice but to forgive him.

"It was like holding the anger toward him was cutting off *my* circulation. I couldn't breathe straight no more. My thoughts were all tainted. It was like I had smoked a whole pack of Kools all at once. And yeah, I used to smoke, by the way.

"Yes, I was fully grown and had a right to feel anything I wanted—even hatred—but it was doing me more bad than good.

"To be honest with you, I didn't decide to forgive Reverend Falls. I decided not to suffocate from holding in all that smoke. I decided I wanted to breathe again. So I let out the bad air. And when I went to take in another breath, I realized that at least then I knew the truth. Truth can hurt at first, but it also makes us free in the end.

"I don't know what the end is for you, Cheryl. I know mine was a rare case. Not everyone can turn the other cheek on some of the things I was slapped with. But when I realized that the truth I took in was really only God trying to open my eyes, the light came on. Heck, the light came in and God did the rest. I can't say what your end will be, but at least, Cheryl, let out the pack of Kools."

Dinner continued without any new words. The only sound was of silver forks hitting Ruthie's good china in a steady rhythm. Eyes avoided contact; only plates held their gaze.

"Excuse me," Yvonne said, interrupting the silence of the big people from the kitchen door. "JoAnne and I are finished eating. Reverend Falls, is it all right if she goes outside with me?"

"Sure, if she'd like, but only for a little while. I think we'll be leaving soon."

"Not before you have a cup of coffee and a slice of my famous chocolate-chocolate cake," Ruthie said, trying to salvage the last shred of dignity she had left for hosting her pastor.

"Oh, I don't know if we should, Sister Boyd," Reverend Falls said.

"I insist."

"Well, Mom, is it okay if we go outside?" Yvonne asked Cheryl, who sat cemented to her seat in a daze. "Mom? Mom!"

"Hmm?"

"Is it okay?"

"Oh. Yeah. It's okay."

Ruthie used Cheryl's words as her cue to excuse herself from the table and head for the antique crystal cake stand on her walnut credenza, bearing her famous chocolate-chocolate cake. The back porch door creaked open and then shut behind the girls.

"JoAnne, what do you think of all that dinner talk about love and forgiveness?"

"I think it's what the Bible says—"

"Of course you do. You're the pastor's kid. What I mean is how do *you* feel about it? Really?"

"I guess I never thought about it much."

"Well, I think it's time you should. We'll both be thirteen this year. We have to start thinking for ourselves, you know. Plus, it seems like your parents have a whole lot to say about it. Sounds like they have a lot of secrets, too?"

"I guess. All I know is that my parents used to argue a lot when I was younger and now they don't. Something must have worked. I just do what I'm told. I don't like to get in trouble."

"Who does? But don't you ever wonder about what's going on? I mean, I think I heard your mom say she used to smoke cigarettes. That's a big deal."

"I didn't hear that. Besides, we're not supposed to snoop on big people's conversations."

"So you just want to make believe you didn't hear that?"

"It's not make believe because I really didn't hear that. It's easier this way, don't you think?"

"No, I—"

"Vonnie. Vonnie," a voice whispered from behind Ruthie's prized rosebush.

"Who is that, Yvonne?" JoAnne asked.

"Daddy!" Yvonne shouted, leaping into Jimmy's arms for the first time in two months.

"Shh. You've got to keep it down, baby girl. Your mom doesn't know I'm here just yet."

"Daddy, I missed you. Where have you been? Mom let me call the number you gave her, but they said you checked out. Were you staying in a hotel, Daddy? Can I come, too?"

"Sweetheart, I've missed you, too. I've missed you so much. How's your summer been so far?"

Jimmy's weather-worn army fatigue jacket seemed out of place on this warm sunny day, yet he shivered like the dead of winter was within him.

"It's been pretty good so far. I get to stay up late with Granny."

"What she got you doing that for?"

"So we can sit on the porch and talk."

"What you two got in common so much that it keeps you up past bedtime?"

"We've got a bunch in common. Granny says we're like the same person in two—I'm just a younger version, that's all. Like two peas in a pod."

"Really? Okay, Vonnie. Daddy's got to go."

"But you just got here."

"I promise to come see you again real soon. Soon as I can. Can you keep this a secret, though? I mean, us talking today?"

"Yes, Daddy."

"I'll tell your mom myself. Just not today, okay?"

"Okay, Daddy. I love you."

"Love you too, baby girl. Now go back to playing with your friend."

Jimmy slipped away as quietly as he had appeared. Within seconds he was a stone's throw away from 1047 Lexington Lane. A stone's throw away from the woman-child he was no longer raising, and miles away from the woman choking on the hurt inside her heart.

Chapter Five

SECRETS OF THE NIGHT

Ruthie arose from a restless night, struggling to make sense of the day before. She pulled on her floral pink housecoat to shield herself from the morning chill as if donning her uniform as the home's caped crusader. Slippers? Check. Glasses? Check.

Somehow the crusader knew the root cause of Sunday's dinner fiasco would be revealed. The true culprit of destruction would be unmasked. She just had to prepare the right approach to unveil it.

A few floorboard creaks toward the bedroom door stirred Papa Boyd enough to turn over in his sleep. He hadn't been an early riser in years, since he retired from Wisconsin Steel. Ruthie continued, pulling the door shut behind her and heading down the dim hallway to the kitchen. Minutes later a pot of Folgers blend percolated a familiar brew throughout the air.

Ruthie credited herself with being the watchman of her home. Man in the house or not, she was last to bed and first to rise. The first hour of the day was her time to reflect on the day before and center her thoughts for the day ahead.

How embarrassing for the pastor and first lady to have such a secret revealed in front of their parishioners, and on the Lord's Day at that! What was worse was having it done at the hand of her eldest and in her own home. What was going on with Cheryl? She really hadn't said a word about Jimmy since the night she moved back home two months before. Ruthie tried over and again to get her to open up, but Cheryl always refused. Maybe she was trying to be strong for Yvonne. Or maybe she was just so hurt that she couldn't find the words to begin to tell her story.

An hour passed before another face emerged from the hibernating brood. It was Sheila getting an early start to her workday, eager to see Bobby for the first time in two days.

"Morning, Mama."

"Hey, Shay."

"Coffee smells good. Are we out of cream?"

"No, I just opened a new bottle of half-and-half. It's in the icebox."

"You want one of these leftover biscuits while I'm in here?"

"Had one already. You help yourself."

"So how'd you sleep last night?"

"I think I flipped over more times than a johnnycake."

"Hmm. I know you sleep light, but that's strange even for you. Something on your mind, Mama?"

"Yeah, yesterday. I don't know what I should be more—angry or embarrassed."

"Oh, that," Sheila said, putting her biscuits in the oven for warming. "Even I was surprised by that one. I didn't know what to say that whole time, so I just kept my mouth shut. I guess Cheryl is more upset about her and Jimmy busting up than she's been letting on. I know I would be. I mean, think about it. Can you imagine putting your dreams on hold over and over again to support a brotha', only to have him let you down over and over again? That's got to be tough. Then, on top of that, now she has to raise a child all alone."

"She's not all alone. She has us."

"I know that, but you know what I mean. He's not around."

"He can't be right now. He's not well. He came back from that war and hasn't been the same. He's out there doing God only knows what. I don't think doctors have a diagnosis for him, let alone a cure."

"I know, but that's a reason, not an excuse. He's not excused from being a husband and father because of that. Those were roles he had before he left here. Cheryl and Yvonne should have always come first to him. They need him."

"Shay, I wish it was that clear-cut, but it isn't. It's more complicated than that. Love usually is. Then throw in a few hand grenades, and you have a real explosion on your hands."

Just then, creaking steps signaled that the third member of the Boyd brood was awake. Cheryl joined them quietly in the kitchen.

"Morning," she said sheepishly.

"Morning," Ruthie said, not quite ready for a confrontation. "Where's that grandbaby of mine?"

"I told her to wake up about twenty minutes ago," Cheryl said. "No sense in sleeping her whole summer away."

"Let me go see what I can do," Ruthie said, welcoming the early exit to better prepare her strategy. "Oh, there's a few leftover biscuits in the fridge you might want. I'll make Maypo for Yvonne when I get her to come downstairs. Evaporated milk with extra sugar, just the way she likes it."

"Thanks, Mama, but you know you're gonna spoil her."

"Oh, that's just as good as done. She *is* my only grandbaby, you know."

The two sisters were left alone—Cheryl hoping to avoid any rebroadcasts of yesterday's debacle, and Sheila hoping to get her sister to finally open up. Their sisterly bond was one of equal parts input and restraint, each respecting the other's right to be wrong.

"How'd you sleep, Cheryl?"

"Average, I guess."

"Hmm. You sure? I thought I heard you up in the middle of the night."

"You *are* Ruthie Boyd's daughter after all, aren't you? House watchdog number two, huh?"

"No, I'm no watchdog. I just got up to use the bathroom and I thought I heard you crying, that's all. I was going to peep in on you then, but I figured maybe you needed some time alone."

"Huh."

"Are you okay, Cheryl? I mean really, girl, what was all that about yesterday?" Sheila asked, spreading butter and then grape jam on two biscuits.

"I'm just fine. Nothing I can't handle."

"If there's something on your mind, you can tell me, Big Sis. It won't go any further if you don't want it to. I just want to make sure you're okay."

"I'm cool."

"You know, I caught the tail end of *60 Minutes* last night. And they aired a piece about the untold effects of Vietnam on local families. This one lady said her husband came back half crazy, throwing things, cursing, starting fistfights. She even woke up in the middle of the night with him choking her. He thought she was a spy. Can you imagine, your own husband turning on you like that? Any man doing that, period, let alone your husband."

"Imagine that."

"I just found that intriguing . . . I hope that if you ever experienced anything like that you'd feel like you could tell us, at least one of us."

"Uh-huh. Free as a bird," Cheryl murmured. "Leave the oven on for me."

"I just remember the night you and Yvonne showed up here a few months back. You were crying like you'd seen a monster. But you never told us exactly what happened, Cheryl. Something happened that you need to get off your chest. If not, you'll be no better off than Jimmy is right now, walking around like a ghost, carrying all those secrets and ugly things he saw over there. It's like he's the living dead. I think you've seen some pretty ugly things yourself, but for some reason you still want to cover them up. It's like you're hiding in broad daylight."

"Okay, Shay."

"I don't mean to pry. I just don't like seeing you this way."

"Okay already!"

"Here's sleeping beauty," Ruthie said, walking in just in time with Yvonne.

"I tell you, it never ceases to amaze me how one word from you pushes the on switch for this girl," Cheryl said. "Did you wash up, Yvonne?"

"Yes, Mama," Yvonne muttered, still half asleep.

"Fresh underwear?"

"Yes, Mama."

"Man, Cheryl. Give the girl a break," Sheila defends.

"I have to check with this one. She still has some of those tomboyish ways of hers to break. I don't want my daughter smelling like some jungle boogie. That's just plain mannish."

"Be that as it may, she's still a smart young lady. Aren't you, Yvonne?"

"Yes, Auntie Sheila. And a clean one, too."

"Ha! Well, let me head on out. I've got first shift at the store."

"Good ole Monkey Wards. See if they have any Sheba pantyhose on sale for me," Cheryl said, creating a new train of thought away from her point of avoidance. "I need coffee or just a half shade lighter. Get me the average height please, ma'am. Here's a dollar."

"It's Montgomery Ward, thank you very much."

"Monkey, Montgomery, I don't care who he was. Just pick up me a pair of café au lait in large," Ruthie concurred, pulling out a dollar from her housecoat pocket. "Get the short length. If not, I can always tuck the toe underneath. I need to make sure I have enough room for these hips of mine. Better yet, get me some stockings. That'll work out even better."

"What's the difference between pantyhose and stockings, Granny? They both look the same on your legs to me."

"Grandbaby, that's exactly the difference. They look the same on the legs, but pantyhose cover your bottom, while stockings stop at your girdle. My hips need a little more reinforcement than a lil' pair of pantyhose can muster up."

"Those are good ole childbearing hips, Mama," Cheryl said.

"Well, they've long served their purpose, then. Wish I could pass 'em on to the next generation."

"Don't look at me. I've got my hands full with Yvonne. It's been almost thirteen years out the gate for me. Don't think I have a second round in me anywhere. Plus, I don't have much in the hip department. I think that gene skipped me. Maybe Miss Sheila will have some use for them in the near future. After all, she's the one who has those Boyd hips."

"I don't think so. Only thing Miss Sheila's got time to think about now is hitting those books," Ruthie said.

"Thanks so much for speaking of me like I'm not even in the room," Sheila said.

"Any time, Lil' Sis."

"Granny, what shade of pantyhose do I need?"

"Girl, what are you wondering about pantyhose for, anyway?" Cheryl asked.

"Cheryl, you know the girl's 'bout to be a teenybopper any day now," Ruthie said. "It's about time she'd concern herself with that and a whole lot more ladylike stuff."

"We'll cross that bridge when we come to it. For now, she's still a girl. My little brown girl. And her little hips are just fine resting above those fancy nylon socks I bought six pairs of for two dollars at Sears last week."

"Okay, enough already about the hips and slips. I'll pick up the pantyhose and the stockings on my break," Sheila said, heading out the kitchen doorway. "I'll see you guys later this evening. Bobby's picking me up today. I think he'll take me out to dinner, too."

"Well la-di-da," Cheryl teased. "What's with Bobby? I thought you said the proper name was Robert? When are you going to invite him over for Sunday dinner?"

"I'm not paying you any mind, Cheryl. Besides, Sunday dinner is a little too eventful these days," Sheila said walking toward the front door. "Oh, wait a minute. I almost forgot. Yvonne, I've got something for you."

"What is it, Auntie Sheila?"

"It's your birthday present, that's what. I know I'm a couple weeks early, but I'm just so excited for you to have it. Plus it was the perfect one, and I was able to use my discount at the store."

"I don't know that she's ready for something that personal, Sheila," Cheryl said.

"Cheryl, we already talked about this and you agreed. Plus, it's time for Yvonne to have something all to herself. She's old enough now, you know," Sheila said, pulling the package out of her work bag.

"Here, Yvonne. Open it."

Yvonne eagerly ripped opened the comic-strip-wrapped square, preserving only the pretty red bow. It reminded her of Christmas.

Bow off? Check. Paper off? Check.

"It's a book. What's the name of it, Auntie Sheila?"

"It's the story of you."

"Huh?"

"It's a diary, Yvonne. It's your story. You can write anything about your life that you want in there, all your hopes and dreams, your fears, even your secrets. It's all about you."

Suddenly the red bow paled next to the green leatherbound memoir-to-be. Finally a treasure of her own, like those treasured rocking chairs Ruthie shared with her on the front porch each night. Something she could grow to cherish, learn to love. Better yet, something that would teach her that she needed to be cherished and be loved.

"Thank you, Auntie Shay! And look, there's even a lock. I don't own anything with a lock and key. I don't even have a key to the house. I finally have my very own key. And it's all just for me, right, Auntie Sheila?"

"Yes, girly. It's all for you. For your eyes only. Make sure to keep it in a safe place," Sheila said, eyeing Cheryl.

"Now, I don't know about that for-your-eyes-only business, Shay," Cheryl interjected. "We never discussed that. I'm still the girl's mother and I may need to check up on her from time to time."

"Don't you dare," Ruthie said. "It's 'bout time this child had something of her own without you snooping every other second. Besides, I let you and Shay have diaries around that age. I don't see no harm in it at all."

"No, it might not harm anything in the long run, but it sure might hurt some things along the way."

"Oh, Cheryl. You sound older than Mama. No offense, Mama."

"Gee, thanks," Ruthie said.

"I'm just saying. She sounds paranoid or something. It's really not that serious, Sis. Heck, she's practically a teenager. You have to give her some leeway."

"That's exactly why I want to keep a close watch. I remember what I was thinking and hiding when I was a teenager."

"Oh, now you think it's worth a mother intruding on a budding woman every once in a while. I sure wish you could go back in time and tell that to yourself," Ruthie said. "Anyway, I say let the young lady be a young lady."

"I have a say, right?"

"Yes, Granny's Baby."

"Hey, thanks, Mama," Cheryl said. "What am I, chopped liver?"

"Speak your mind, child."

"I think it's great, and I love it. Thank you, Auntie Shay. Now I have something to hold my secrets safe and sound from any and everyone else. No one else has a right to it, not even Mom!"

"See what you've started already, Shay?"

"Now, you didn't mean any harm, did you, my sweet niece?"

"No, not at all. I love it! Thanks, Mom, for letting me keep it."

"I still don't know if I like the idea of her keeping secrets at the age of twelve."

"Cheryl, the girl will be a teenager in two weeks. Cool out," Sheila said. "She'll be physically stepping into her womanhood any day now, and you know what I mean. So, it's time. Let her have something of her own in the world. Besides, everyone *else* around here has secrets."

"Okay, Shay," Cheryl said through clenched teeth.

"Thank you, Auntie Sheila!"

"You're welcome, Sweetie. Okay, now let me make sure I've got enough tokens for the bus. I'm really gone this time, y'all."

"Bye Auntie Shay," Yvonne said, giving her a kiss on the cheek and a squeeze around the neck.

Yvonne was excused to eat her breakfast at the dining room table for a change. Meanwhile, awkward silence grew with each echo of Sheila's platform shoes toward the front door. The remaining Boyd women sat at the kitchen table, sensing a big-people conversation brewing—one stronger than their morning coffee.

"So how'd you sleep, Miss Cheryl?"

The Miss handle on any of their names was Ruthie's unspoken code for "So you think you're finally grown enough to disrespect my house?"

"Fine."

"You know something? Monday mornings can be draining sometimes, especially when you feel you didn't get quite right with the good Lord the day before.

"I had a pretty restless night," Ruthie continued. "Just couldn't seem to catch more than forty minutes of shuteye at a time. I just— just didn't feel settled in my spirit, you know?"

Ruthie had baited her hook and was fishing for a bite of conversation. So far, there were no takers. Cheryl sat perched on the edge of her seat, taking slow, purposeful bites of her buttered biscuits. Her lips only grasped for the brim of her favorite navy-trimmed coffee mug.

"You know, I just wonder sometimes how much account the good Lord takes of the things we've done the night before," Ruthie said. "I'm so glad that we gain new mercies each and every morning. I just wonder if He allows us to double up on occasion."

"You just wonder, huh?"

"Yes, I just wonder."

"You know what I wonder sometimes, Mother? I wonder if He even hears anything I say at all. He sure hasn't seemed to be listening to me much lately."

"He's always listening, child. Don't you know there's a record on high of every word we say?"

"Okay, just cut to the chase already, Mama, and stop beating around the bush."

"I'm not beating around any bushes. I'm just trying to figure out what's gotten into you. What was that all about yesterday, Cheryl?"

"What was what all about, Mama?"

"Oh, now who's beating around the bush? That conversation with Pastor Falls, that's what I'm talking about."

"That, Mother, was about a grown woman speaking her heart and her mind to her pastor. Is that all right with you?"

"It would be plenty all right with me if it were done decently and in order. Nothing about that was decent or in order. You had no right interrogating the man of God and his wife out in the open like that. And what was worse was that you did it in my house, when they were my invited guests! They were in *my* home, Cheryl, eating my food! How dare you think it was fair to grill them like two common thieves? It was completely humiliating and embarrassing."

"They didn't seem to mind it. Matter of fact, I even got a second sermon out of the whole deal! So who was really humiliated and embarrassed, Mother: them, or you? I don't think you're nearly as concerned about their feelings as you are about your own! You walk around like you're so tight with the Lord that there's barely room in your heart for your own children!"

"How dare you?"

"How dare I? How dare you? How dare you pretend that any of this was ever about them? It's all about you. Your all-white-wearing, Mother's-board, picture-perfect image was shattered and you just can't stand it!"

"Now you've really gone too far, Missy!"

"Oh, have I, Mom? Are you trying to silence me again? It's so funny. On the one hand, everyone around here wants me to talk about things. Get it off your chest, Cheryl. You'll feel better, Cheryl. But no sooner do I open my mouth than people are on standby, telling me to shut up! Which is it, Mother?"

"You've either lost your cotton-picking mind or you have amnesia, because I know you've forgotten who you're talking to, girl! I want you to talk. I want you to get things off your chest, but not at everyone else's expense. Why are you always on-guard?"

"It's not all the time. It's hardly any of the time. That's why folks keep asking me to talk. Then as soon as I open my mouth, someone's telling me to shut it! No wonder I have so much pressure built up inside! Then I go to the place where I should be able to get a load off my chest, and I'm shut down there, too! It's like I'm wrong when I'm wrong, and when I'm right."

Just then the internal pressure grew beyond what Cheryl could contain. For months she had held her emotions intact like a good Boyd woman should. For months, her emotional Hoover Dam had secured the self-made fort around her heart. Atop that were the self-imposed embankments guarding her from the conflicting voices of other people. On one day, people would say, "Speak up,

Cheryl. We can't help you if we don't know what's wrong." The next day it was, "No one likes a pity party, Cheryl."

Now, in one volcanic moment, those opposing pressures had become too great for Cheryl to bear. Her floodgates broke wide open and out flowed polluted waters, stale waters, drowning her face like a river after a winter thaw. The reservoir of her soul had reached its breaking point. Her belly ached with the press of each ear-piercing scream.

Yvonne stood frozen at the kitchen doorway. Ruthie sat in utter silence. Neither Yvonne or Ruthie had seen Cheryl cry since Jimmy went off to Vietnam, and never before like this. Through her staccato cries, Cheryl mustered up enough breath to call out for help.

"I've tried to do right by everyone around me. I've tried to respect your house, even when I had to leave my own. I've tried to respect the preacher, even though he's done more wrong than me. I've tried. I've even tried to respect my husband, but now he's walking around town like some crazed zombie! Who's gonna respect me? Who's gonna honor me? Huh? Who's gonna give me the chance to have my say? I'm not a robot. I'm not! I have feelings, too; and I have a right to feel them and show them just like everybody else! And no one gets to say whether they're right or wrong, good or bad, because they're not the ones feeling them. I am! I am! Or better yet, maybe I just don't want to feel anything anymore!"

Now, glancing at a previously unnoticed butcher knife on the table, Cheryl impulsively secured it with her right hand and moved with a determined stroke toward her left.

In one swift move, Ruthie rose to restrain Cheryl's right arm with all her might, holding back the very hand of death from her eldest child.

"No!" she shouted with all her strength.

Heartbeats raced. Hands trembled. No blood. No blood. No blood.

As if in sync for a second childbirth, Ruthie and Cheryl took in one deep breath together, Ruthie's in relief that the hand of the reaper was stilled, Cheryl's in utter defeat that he was. Ruthie stood in silence, her hands slowly removing her daughter's weapon of convenience. Cheryl's fists clenched, her chest heaved, and her belly swelled with new rivers to release. Polluted tears gave way to screams, and screams slowly gave way to a healing stream.

Yvonne, frozen at the kitchen door, felt compelled to reach out to the hurting little girl she now saw inside her adult mother.

"I respect you, Mama. Don't go. I'm sorry. I'm sorry. I respect you, Mama. Don't go," Yvonne said, shedding a single stream of her own.

"Yvonne, give your Mama some space. Why don't you go out front for a bit?" Ruthie finally said. "Maybe play with one of your friends."

"Huh? Mama needs me. It's too early for them to come outside, anyway."

"Don't worry about that now."

"I just wanted to—"

"Just go, I said. Go!"

"But—but—I just wanted—"

"I said go!"

Cheryl's pollution was no longer her own. Her chemical spill had now silently infected the roots of a budding woman who had not yet learned how to filter out her mother's pain. Feeling that she was in the way of the big people, yet somewhat responsible for their pain, Yvonne left, confused by Cheryl's tears and Ruthie's words.

Two sets of footsteps crossed paths in the hallway: Yvonne's as she reluctantly did as she was told, and the oblivious Mr. Pratt's as he made a brief appearance for his one true vice.

"Good morning, Yvonne . . . Good morning ladies," he said, entering the kitchen. "How's everyone this fine Monday morning? I'm just stopping in for my morning cup of coffee, if it's no trouble, Ms. Ruthie."

Still standing over Cheryl's shoulder, Ruthie nodded in agreement as her only response.

"I just simply can't resist the smell of coffee in the morning. It just gets me moving," he said, reaching for a Styrofoam cup and the coffeepot. "And your blend, Ms. Ruthie. I tell you, it's simply heaven-sent. I'll have some cream and sugar, too, if you don't mind, Ms. Ruthie."

Once again, Ruthie's affirming nod was enough.

"Mmm-hmm. Sheer heaven, I say. Well, nice chatting with you ladies. Have a wonderful day."

Mr. Pratt left as seemingly oblivious as when he entered, clad in his plaid suitcoat with elbow patches even on a hot summer's day.

Ruthie slowly placed her hands on Cheryl's shoulders, having just then found enough strength to move her own limbs.

Cheryl's actions were indeed poignant, but her words were common poison for Ruthie. Ruthie had developed an immunity to them from years of standing guard over her own troubled waters. The only difference was that Ruthie had managed to keep standing guard over her emotions even when she didn't want to. More so, Ruthie was sad that, unbeknownst to her, her daughter had attempted the same stance of resistance. Perhaps the break in Cheryl's emotional dam would give Ruthie the courage to break out of her own.

"I heard you, Cheryl. Mama heard you."

In one clean swoop, Ruthie helped Cheryl rise from the table and take baby steps toward the second floor.

"I'm tired, Mama. I'm so, so tired."

"Mama knows, Cheryl. Mama knows."

The two made their way upstairs to the room Cheryl shared with Yvonne. Cheryl's weak arms fell limp at her sides. Ruthie's arms supported Cheryl's waist, as if she was teaching her to walk all over again. Slowly they climbed the creaking staircase. Ruthie pushed wide the oak door. The floorboards gave way to their tandem steps. Cheryl laid across the bed sideways, as if the walk had taken the very last ounce of her strength. Ruthie removed Cheryl's shoes and shrouded her with the family's yellow and blue patchwork quilt that had been draped over an old parson's chair. The quilt had always brought Cheryl comfort as a little girl.

Ruthie tucked in her woman-child for a long nap and drew the shades. Sitting on the bed's edge, Ruthie stroked Cheryl's hair while humming melodies only the good Lord could understand. She prayed for peace in her daughter's mind, comfort, and strength for the journey yet to come. She prayed for her own strength to somehow show Cheryl the way out of a place she had yet to escape herself.

Chapter Six

CONFESSIONS

Dear Diary,

Hi. My name is Yvonne Carpenter, but I'm really a Boyd. My Auntie Sheila just gave you to me for my 13th birthday. It's coming up in 2 weeks. I'm so happy to have you. Finally, I have something I can call my very own. No big people telling me what I can or can't say. It's my turn now. Every time I open you to a new page, I'll remember that.

The big people have so many problems, but they try not to show it around me. I still see it, though. I just do. Mama's crying right now because she's trying too hard to be big. It's okay to take a break sometimes. Today I heard Granny scream, "No!" Then I saw Granny holding Mama's hand on the kitchen table. Mama was holding a butcher knife. I think she misses Daddy a whole lot. She just hasn't said so. I think she wants to see him as much as I do. She's just trying to stay big and won't say so. I hate to see her cry. I wanted to hug her to make her feel better like she does when I'm crying, but she ignored me and Granny told me to leave. I feel sad now, too. I just wanted to hug her. Maybe when I see Daddy again, I can tell him how sad Mama is and we can go back home. He showed up yesterday, but nobody knows but me, him, and JoAnne Falls and I made her pinkie swear not to tell a soul.

Then Auntie Sheila's worried about her boyfriend Bobby. At least I think so. She's always saying something without saying anything. It's like she knows something's not right but she doesn't want to look at it. Like she's trying to talk herself out of what she already knows. I guess she's already taking a break from being big. No one else knows but me and you.

And Granny is just trying to help everybody at 1047 Lexington Lane. That's where I live, at least for now. I love being with Granny, but maybe soon me and Mama can go back home. Oh, I already have a secret to tell you. <u>I'm going to find Daddy</u>! I've got to go for now.

Love,
Yvonne

Ruthie checked in on Yvonne just as her first journal entry came to an end. Yvonne turned and rose from the top porch step. She was sitting there rather than risking any more conflicts by sitting uninvited in one of the sacred rocking chairs.

"Grandbaby, why don't you see if Thelma can come out to play? Tell her mother I need to run out for a while and to keep an eye on you. I'll give you both some change for the candy store. How's that sound?"

"Okay, I guess," Yvonne said with a hint of uncertainty in her voice. "But it's not even noon."

"I know it's still too early for Thelma to come outside. That's why I said to tell her mom I need to go out for a bit. She'll understand."

"Why do I still need a babysitter? I'm almost thirteen."

"As for a babysitter, I know you're not a baby, but you're still my baby," Ruthie said mildly, making up for her snippy response in the kitchen. "So I'd rather have an extra pair of eyes looking out for you while I'm gone."

"Where are you going? Why can't I just go with you?"

"Look here, Lil' Shadow Man, I'll report back to base at a decent hour."

"Or I could just stay and look after Mama."

"Your Mama's getting some much-needed rest, and we're gonna keep it that way."

"Okay, Granny. Let me go hide my diary first."

"Hide away. Just be quick about it and don't wake your Mama."

"Is she all right?"

"She will be. She's just really tired and needs to rest a while. I think we all do. Too much commotion this early in the day."

"Was Mama trying to hurt herself?"

"Child, what are you talking about? Of course she wasn't. She was just letting out a little steam, that's all. Even I've tried to do that before. But then we take a nap, a really long nap. And when we wake up, we realize that we really did wake up, and we're grateful.

"Now, come inside so you can hide your little treasure book, and I can finish getting ready."

In the brief moments that passed, Ruthie dressed for the day and presented the remaining biscuits with syrup to Papa Boyd, who had finally emerged from hibernation. The two exchanged their routine niceties as he settled in on the enclosed back porch. His old black and white TV was tuned to back-to-back episodes of *The Lone Ranger.*

Yvonne walked toward the room she shared with Cheryl, but saw the door closed. Afraid to disturb her mother's sleep or to open more wounds, she decided on a detour. Yvonne stepped inside of the neatly kept solitude of Sheila's room as her escape route. She began searching for the perfect place. Behind the headboard? No. Maybe underneath the chest of drawers? Not there, either. What about the closet floor right behind the bottom row of Chernin's shoeboxes? Perfect.

Yvonne often explored her Auntie Sheila's room. Its glass-topped chest of drawers was neatly decorated with crystal bottles and decanters of perfume. Sweet, floral fragrances, each one like a unique bouquet of lilies, lilacs, or roses. To the right sat a baby doll—her single childhood heirloom. Beside it was the genuine silver hairbrush and mirror set passed down from Ruthie; Cheryl had her mother's single strand of pearls. On the left sat a satin-covered jewelry box with a ballerina who danced whenever someone opened the lid.

Yvonne explored each knickknack as if for the first time, gently lifting it from its place. She frequently visited Sheila's world, imagining herself to be like Shay: independent, smart, ambitious. Then, ever so carefully, she replaced each item as if she had never been there. Yvonne could easily spend an hour playing this game of discovery, but not today. Ruthie was sure to be expecting her quick return.

Yvonne gave one last glance to ensure that everything was back in its rightful place. She pulled Sheila's door closed and lightly crept past Cheryl's hallowed door. She paused only to listen for her mother's breath sounds, thinking if she could hear them, she would know Cheryl was all right. Sound check? Affirmative.

Ruthie gathered three of her most valuable assets: her pocketbook, glasses, and Yvonne, then headed toward the front door.

"Yvonne, here's a dollar for you and your friend to share. Now don't you go crazy with that penny candy, child. People don't have money to go carrying you off to the dentist for a sore tooth, you know. I'd just as well tie a string on the doorknob and pull it myself."

"Whoa. I *thought* I wanted some candy."

"Here, just—I mean . . . I'll see you when I get back. Now don't you go sassing Thelma's mama. Not everybody knows how to interpret that tongue of yours, you hear me?"

"Yes, ma'am."

"I'll be back in time for a late lunch, so don't go eating over there, either."

"Yes, ma'am."

"Vonnie, you don't have to ma'am me. I don't mean to be snippy with you. I just—I—Granny needs to take her walk, that's all."

Yvonne grabbed her jar of marbles from the doorway étagère, then walked obediently to Thelma's next door. Ruthie stood at the top step, waiting for her neighbor to emerge. Yvonne pointed toward her as she explained Ruthie's request. A raised hand from Thelma's mother and a hand-wave of thanks from Ruthie were enough to seal the temporary exchange. Ruthie headed down the weather-worn slanted steps, moving closer to her goal.

EBBS AND FLOWS

Ruthie made it a point to spend at least one afternoon alone each week. It was rather early for her break, but with all the recent drama, she truly needed the premature reprieve. She always put so much time into her home, her family, and church that she figured the good Lord would be pleased with her taking a little time for herself. This day, she *knew* He would.

Some days she went window shopping at Sears or Wieboldt's. Other days she opted for an L ride downtown just to see the sights. This particular day, she decided to people watch in the park a half-mile up the street. There she could sort through her thoughts, or rather, soar right past them.

Ruthie's favorite pastime was sitting and reminiscing about the good ole days. She could daydream for hours about the times when Forty-Seventh Street was really something to see. There were late night parties at Palm's Tavern, concerts at the Apollo Theater, and even the impromptu jazz and blues sets after a show at the Metro. She remembered riding the red streetcars down Forty-Seventh Street to Cottage Grove, and how neighbors would have quarter parties and chitlin struts just to pay their rent. Times were tight moneywise back then, but people stayed together and helped one another. She recalled her family's third-floor apartment down the street from Earnestine Gibson. She especially remembered the New Year's Eve night when she met Monroe Jackson. Ruthie never believed in love at first sight before then, and never had again.

Monroe Jackson was tall, slim, and confident. His smooth, dark brown complexion was a welcome, blended contrast to his bright Southern smile. His gait was balanced and poised, like he came into the world already a grown man, practiced and polished. He wore his pride on his shoulders like some fancy war medal. It made good sense, too, seeing that he was fresh on his way to the military once he finished high school that June. And he was smart. He avoided the draft by volunteering for service, thinking he would get a lighter duty than combat. So far, he had played his hand just right. For now he was to be a serviceman for the navy's latest fleet, and was six months away from reporting for duty at Great Lakes.

Monroe had a house full of siblings and was the eldest of eight. His mother stayed home to wean and rear her children. His father was a porter on the local Burlington Northern Line. Monroe was determined not to follow in his father's footsteps, though. It wasn't that his father's work wasn't honorable; Monroe simply wasn't the type to let life lock him down. He saw no sense in obligating himself to one piece of land when the whole world was set before him. Monroe had his own wings. So it was more than a hint of confidence that he carried into Tommy Brown's party in New Year's Eve of 1940. He was a go-getter, a person who knew what he wanted out of life, the one all his friends followed like a guiding star.

Monroe and Ruthie always sparred about who spotted who first. Yet they both agreed it was just one of those things that happened right in sync, right in time. It was clear that Monroe thought it would be shameful for such a fine prospect to go through life all alone, and Ruthie thought the same.

The basement was just barely lit by the fluorescent pink lights beaming from the secondhand jukebox. Someone had selected a Muddy Waters record to fill up the dance floor. There was a built-in bar and only a few hand-carved bar stools, emphasizing the standing room only.

Ruthie caught a glimpse of Monroe out of the corner of her eye, and her heart was racing a mile a minute. Of course, she needed to be properly introduced. Ruthie's friend Earnestine was dating Tommy, who was home on leave from the navy, so she thought to have them run interference. Just as she turned to catch their eye on the dance floor, she felt a warm presence over her left shoulder.

"Excuse me, Miss. Is this seat taken?" Monroe asked Ruthie.

"Um, only if you sit in it."

"What ya' having?"

"Oh, I'm not a drinker."

"Good for you. Neither am I. I'm having a root beer. I never really caught the taste for the real deal. Tried plenty of times, but no dice.

"So, what's a lady like you doing sitting at a bar alone if you don't drink? Oh, I know. You must be on the hunt for Mr. Right."

"No hunting here," Ruthie said, holding her composure. "Actually, I'm here with my girlfriend. She's more boy crazy than I'll ever be. Always has been. Besides, this isn't a real bar anyway."

"Is that her over there, hugged up with Tommy Brown?"

"Over by the jukebox?" Ruthie asked, spinning around in her stool. "Yeah, that's Miss Teenybopper herself. They've been an item since the ninth grade. Well, we were in ninth, but he was a sophomore.

"You know, I'm not much for bar stools either," Ruthie continued, looking for a way to overcome her jitters. "It was just the only place to sit."

"Looks to me like you've got the best seat in the house. All perched up high like a nightingale in a treetop. For someone who's not boy crazy, you sure got yourself up high and mighty on the shelf. Easy to spot, I'd say."

"I'm a lady, Mister. I'm just here for the music."

"Oh, I was just joshing with ya'. It's obvious you're a lady. I can tell by the way you carry yourself.

"Pardon my manners, ma'am. Allow me to introduce myself. I'm Monroe Jackson, originally out of Tennessee."

"Really? What part?"

"Well, now, where's your manners? I don't go giving out my family history to perfect strangers, you know. I am a Southern gentleman, after all."

"You're funny. Pardon my manners. I'm Ruthie. Ruthie Tucker."

"Nice to make your acquaintance, Ms. Tucker," Monroe said, reaching for a handshake.

On contact, Ruthie knew something special was about to happen to her because of Monroe Jackson. She thought he was simply a fine specimen. Tall, six feet at least. He carried broad shoulders. Not overwhelmingly broad, but just enough to fill out his starched white shirt and blue and black argyle sweater. He had strong, stern arms, good for everything from hard work to holding her. She was entranced by his deep, sincere brown eyes and bright smile. Beyond that, there was something more. Something deep within her belly knew she wanted to know him forever.

"Ms. Ruthie. Ms. Ruthie. Ms. Ruthie? You got any sugar I could borrow for my evening cup of coffee? I'm plumb out. I'll make it up to you with the rent next week." Ruthie's boarder, Mr. Pratt, saw her sitting alone on the park bench and thought it as good a time as any to tend to a little housekeeping.

"I'm sorry, Mr. Pratt. Did you say something?" Ruthie said, gradually coming back to reality. "What did you ask me for?"

"Some—some sugar, ma'am," Mr. Pratt said as he looked at her over his glasses. "That's all. I'm plumb out. I need it for my coffee. I'll make it up to you with next week's rent."

"There's no need for that, Mr. Pratt. Besides, I keep telling you that you get one meal a day with your rent, and coffee anytime it's available. It's room *and* board. You just only take advantage of my offer on Sundays," Ruthie said. "Why is that, anyway? Do you have enough food throughout the week?"

"Oh, I have. I have a-plenty, Ms. Ruthie. I have a-plenty," he said, studying a crack in the sidewalk. "I just need sugar for my coffee, that's all. Coffee's no good without it."

"I'm sorry to be so forward, Mr. Pratt. I didn't mean to hurt your feelings."

"No harm done, Ms. Ruthie. Besides, my feelings have been hurt so much through the years, I don't think I have much hurt left in me, anyhow." He pulled his glasses back in place on either side. "Never you mind about the sugar. I can make do without it."

"Not at all. There's plenty at home in the kitchen. Take all you need." She stood. "Come on, Mr. Pratt. I've daydreamed long enough for one day. I'll walk back with you."

"Well, truth be told, I really don't *need* sugar. I need air. I need water. I need a safe place to lay my head. Sugar is just something I want. It makes my life a little sweeter, that's all."

"Well, in my book, that's definitely a need. I think every life needs to be a little sweeter. I could use a five-pound bag of life sweetener myself, especially on today."

"You're too kind, Ms. Ruthie. I'll just have enough for my evening cup of coffee today, and I'll be out of your way."

"You're never in my way, Mr. Pratt. Your face is always a welcome sight."

"Thanks, Ms. Ruthie. I'll make it up to you in next week's rent."

Ruthie saw no sense in telling Mr. Pratt not to add an extra fifty cents to his rent. He would do it anyway. That was just the way Mr. Pratt was with her, with anybody.

Mr. Pratt always held a distant gaze as if the veil of death had come so close to his heart, it left a shadow on his face. He grew nervous when speaking to people and often practiced what he wanted to say. Sometimes he remained stuck on the same rehearsed lines over and over again.

Out of all the ones living at 1047 Lexington Lane, Mr. Pratt had suffered the most hurt and pain. In Korea, he saw a fellow soldier blown up after stepping on a live grenade. Two days later, he got a telegram saying that his mother had died suddenly in her sleep. Then, once he made it back to the States and tried to make a go of life, he lost his wife, their five-year-old daughter, and everything he owned in a house fire in Forsyth County, Georgia. Folks speculated whether it was retaliation for his attempt to desegregate the town. Something in him broke after that, and he was never the same.

Being around the Boyd family, any family, helped him heal a bit, but their presence still reminded him of his loss. Yet he pressed his way, an attribute that made others feel shame for not trying to do the same. He came to the Boyd home once he decided to settle to the north; a room was all he could afford. Moreover, he felt an unexplained comfort around his Ruthie, as if she could somehow fix him or at least keep him from breaking apart any more.

People weren't taking on boarders so much these days, but there was something about Mr. Pratt that made him worth the risk to Ruthie, the investment even. He was a quiet man. Mostly kept to himself, other than volunteering here and there at the veterans' hall. He only asked for a little conversation every now and then. That was about all his heart or mind could handle anyway.

Ruthie and Mr. Pratt strolled toward the park entrance, making light conversation about how well Ruthie's yellow rosebush had bloomed in comparison to the park's patchy buds. They exchanged hellos and how-do-you-dos with passersby and even with Mr. Joe, who was just opening his tavern for his lunchtime crowd.

"Ms. Ruthie, pleasure seeing you out this sunshiny day," Mr. Joe said.

"More a pleasure to be seen. How's business these days?"

"'Bout the same, I suppose. Someone always needs a quick bite to eat."

"Better yet, someone always wants a quick nip to drink, huh?"

"Oh, Ms. Ruthie, it's just a matter of supply and demand. The people demand it, so I supply it. I'm not forcing anything on them."

"Never said you were. I'm not judging a man's livelihood, that's the Lord's work. I'm just making small talk. Good day, Mr. Joe."

"Same to you."

Mr. Pratt remained silent other than a nod and slight tip of the army hat he always wore. Walking away a bit, he regained his voice.

"Ms. Ruthie, I tell you, you know how to be a lady and still hold your own with the best of them. I never took hold to strong drink, ma'am. Would've been real easy to, but I just never did."

"I can say the same thing. Had plenty reason to, just never did. The way I see it, we all have free choice. We can choose our work, our spouse, even our house. Mr. Joe made some different choices, that's all. Who's to say that I wouldn't have chosen differently if I hadn't met up with the Lord when I did? Life sure has been crazy enough to justify taking another pathway; I just didn't have the heart to do it."

"Ms. Ruthie, you're nothing but heart. You just chose to let the right path determine your heartbeat."

"I tried to, Mr. Pratt. I tried to."

DAYDREAMERS

After a pit stop at the school playground, Yvonne and Thelma began their unsuspecting three-block walk to the candy store.

"I already know what I'm getting," Yvonne said.

"What's that?" Thelma asked.

"I'm getting two Slo Pokes, some nut chews, twelve pieces of wine candy, and a bag of Jay's potato chips."

"Make sure you leave enough money for me to get my Black Cow and a Clark bar."

"I know. I know. Hey, wait a minute. Do you see that fella at the corner? He looks a lot like my Auntie Sheila's boyfriend, Bobby."

"Who are you talkin' about, the guy in the short-sleeved checkered shirt? The one coming out of the laundromat?"

"Yeah, him. Let's walk up a little," Yvonne said, looking closer with each step. "That *is* him.

"Hey, Bobby!" Yvonne shouted, waving at him.

The young man looked up instinctively upon hearing his name, but quickly turned away, placing his sole focus on loading the backseat of his black Nova with four bags of freshly laundered clothes.

"Bobby?" Yvonne said again, this time puzzled by his vacant response.

Suddenly, he opened his passenger-side door. A young woman walked out of the laundromat, greeted him with a single kiss on the lips, and settled into the front seat. Once Bobby closed her door, he rushed over to the driver's side and made a quick U-turn onto the main road. A ripped Pepsi bumper sticker was the last glimpse Yvonne saw of Bobby's car.

"Wow! Did you see him kiss that lady on the mouth?" Thelma asked, rhetorically. "I thought you said he was your Auntie Sheila's boyfriend?"

"He is! And I did see him kiss her."

"What are you gonna do? Are you gonna tell her?"

"I know he heard me. I know he saw me," Yvonne said, now questioning herself. "Why would he ignore me? Who was that lady, and why did she kiss him that way?"

"Looks like trouble in paradise to me, Yvonne."

"I've got to tell my Auntie Shay. He's cheating on her!"

"Plus, that lady is pretty, Yvonne. Did you see her fancy makeup? She looked like one of those models from *Jet Magazine*, maybe even *Ebony*. She probably smells nice too, like one of those Charlie or Enjoli perfumes in the ads on TV. Did you get a good look at her?"

"Yes, I did," Yvonne said solemnly.

"Did you see that pretty red polka-dot dress she was wearing? She must have pretty clothes, too, and lots of them. Four bags of laundry are a lot to wash for one person at one time, don't you think?"

"Yes, I do." Yvonne's voice lowered with each response.

"So what you gonna do? When are you gonna tell her?"

"I don't know yet. Maybe it wasn't what it looked like, after all."

"What do you mean, it wasn't what it looked like? You just said you saw them together. We both saw the same thing, and what I saw was your auntie's boyfriend, what's-his-name, kissing another lady. And she was wearing a pretty red polka-dot dress. So if that's not what I saw, then maybe I was just daydreaming. And if I was daydreaming, then I know you were daydreaming, too!"

"Maybe."

"Maybe, nothing! You know what you saw, and you've got to do something."

"Come on. Let's just get the candy and get out of here. I'll figure out something later."

The two girls completed their errand and walked back to Thelma's house in silence, their words now suffocated by sugary treats. Yvonne craved for the sweetness to quickly take effect, to be the childhood elixir that numbed her from the big people's pain. The more she consumed it, the more it seemed to work.

* * *

The curved park pathway slowly blended into the crackled sidewalk along Lexington Lane. Ruthie and Mr. Pratt took their last few steps toward the white-framed house in complete silence. Mr. Pratt kept his usual quiet disposition, and Ruthie contemplated what awaited her beyond her home's front door.

"Granny! Granny!" Yvonne shouted from a few houses down.

Yvonne ran toward Ruthie, but stopped just short of an embrace, hoping that her body language wouldn't divulge the secret she now carried.

"Hi, Grandbaby."

"Do you feel better now?"

"Wasn't sick. I just needed some fresh air." She put her arm around Yvonne's shoulders.

"Do you think Mama feels better?"

"I hope so."

Ruthie waved and nodded a thank you to Thelma's mother, who had just stepped out on their front porch. It was Thelma's lunchtime, and perfect timing for Ruthie's return—seeing as how she never liked any child of hers eating at a neighbor's home. It wasn't so much that she didn't trust her neighbors, but she knew it was hard enough for them to feed their own families without throwing in an unexpected mouth here and there.

"Stay here on the porch for a while, Yvonne," Ruthie said. "We'll eat in a few minutes.

"Mr. Pratt, let's get you that sugar you've been wanting for almost an hour."

"Thank you kindly, Sister Boyd," he said, holding open the screen door for her and waiting for his rare entrance through the home's front door. "Yes, Ms. Ruthie. I'd appreciate that kindly, ma'am."

Now inside, Ruthie drew back the pink sheer curtains she'd forgotten to open in her haste to seek solitude. She headed to the kitchen to retrieve Mr. Pratt's sugar, which he graciously accepted before retreating to his room after offering an unrequited greeting to the now sleeping Papa Boyd.

Ruthie prepared four potted-meat sandwiches on wheat, one each for Papa Boyd, herself, Yvonne, and Cheryl.

Ruthie tread quietly up the stairs, a plate in one hand and purposely gripping the stair rail with the other. Making sure Cheryl was still breathing in the aftermath of her tidal wave of emotions was chore enough.

Cheryl was fast asleep—one of those deep sleeps that stops trouble in its tracks simply because a person is no longer mindful of it. The peace on Cheryl's cocoa brown face displayed that she had discovered the best daydream ever, one in which she was not forced to come back to reality.

Respecting Cheryl's own needed solace, Ruthie placed the sandwich on the nightstand by her bed. She gingerly retrieved a glass of water from the washroom, setting it down softly beside Cheryl. Ruthie took one more glance of inspection.

Breathing? Check.

After a quiet descent, Ruthie woke Papa Boyd with a nudge to eat the lunch now on his TV tray. She then grabbed the remaining sandwiches for herself and Yvonne. Deciding to connect with a little more peace now rather than later in the day, Ruthie made her way back to the front porch.

"Yvonne, come join me in the rocking chairs. Let's have lunch out here for a change."

"Is Mama all right?" Yvonne asked, reaching for the sandwich and taking her invited position in the chair.

"Right as rain. She's dreaming. Can't get much better than that, if you ask me."

The two rocked back and forth, the cedar beams creaking against the white wooden porch.

Ruthie, still in a mental state of daydreams, decided to tell Yvonne her story of the two little red birds.

"I wanna tell Granny's Baby a story. Once upon a time, in a land somewhere in the Midwest—"

"You're kidding me, right, Granny? I'm not a baby anymore. Besides, why do stories always start that way?"

"It's my story. So can I tell my story the way I like to tell it?"

"I guess so. It's just corny, that's all."

"Well, I don't think so. Do you want to hear my story or not?"

"Yeah, yeah. Tell me anyway."

"Okay, as I was saying: Once upon a time, in a land somewhere in the Midwest, lived a pair of little red birds. A boy bird and a girl bird. They were inseparable, like little red birds should be. If you'd see one, you'd definitely see the other."

"One day they mistakenly ended up inside a house where there were snakes and other scary, strange things."

"Now you're talking! Things like what?"

"Oh, um, foxes and bigger birds of prey. But they weren't scared because at least they had each other. Together, the two little red birds could do anything."

"So what did they do?"

"They flew under a sink and hid in its cupboard. They were safe, but they weren't free. Just then, some people came in to rescue them and put everything in the house back in order. A woman on the rescue team discovered the two red birds cuddling together under the sink. She asked the other people to hold the door open so the two little red birds could go free."

"So, did they?" Yvonne asked.

"Well, the male little red bird flew out the door. He was so sure that the little girl bird was right behind him, but instead she got distracted by what looked like a male little white bird."

"Ooh. Now, that ain't right!" Yvonne said. "I just might know these birds."

"The little red girl bird snuggled up with the little white bird on the kitchen countertop. She got real close, you know, but the white bird wasn't real. It only looked like a real bird."

"So what was it, then?"

"A salt shaker. Can you believe it? Just a little three-inch salt shaker! By the time the girl bird realized it, the door was closed. It looked like she was separated from her true little red boy bird forever."

"That's terrible."

"I know, but all was not lost. The woman from the rescue team who opened the door the first time noticed that the little red girl bird was still trapped inside. So she had the door opened again, and then the girl bird flew away to freedom."

"Did she find her true little red boy bird?"

"Well, it was just then that the little red boy bird, the real bird, saw that the door to the house was open again. He had been looking, lonely for his little red girl bird, for so long."

"What happened? What happened?"

"To be continued."

"What? You can't do that, Granny!"

"Oh, yes, I can. It's my story, and I can tell it any kind of way I want. It's a cliffhanger, ain't it? *Guiding Light* ain't got nothin' on my storytelling!"

"Where do you get these stories from, anyway?"

"Pieces of my dreams, parts of my realities."

"So could these red birds represent real people, you think?"

"Suppose they could. I suppose they could."

"So, Granny, what would you do if you knew a little girl bird who ended up with a salt shaker instead of a true little boy bird? I mean, would you tell the little girl bird?"

"I guess I would if it could set the girl bird free, but I would try to do what's best for both of the little red birds if I could."

"But, Granny, sometimes it might not work out that way, right?"

"Yes, I suppose you're right again. You're two for two from the wisdom tree today. You're sounding like a chip off the old block.

"I guess you can't win them all. You basically have to play the hand you're dealt. Grandbaby, I tell you, life is like the game Monopoly."

"How so?"

"Everybody's going round and round the game of life, hoping to land on something good like Park Avenue, Broadway, maybe even a get-out-of-jail-free card. What I'd like to see them make is a get-out-of-life-free card!'"

"What do you mean by that, Granny?"

"Well, everyone's so hell-bent on cleaning up what they've messed up, or, better still, looking for a way to cover it up. But the cycle never ends. Just like that Monopoly board, you're bound to end up in a hogpen of mess all over again. Like the Good Book says, you reap what you sow.

"What you put out, you'll get back again," Ruthie said. "It's sort of like a seashore; the same water that drifts out, looking ever so peaceful, will eventually come crashing back at the shore. My hope is to be free of all the mess for good, to have all the muck and mire gone once and for all. I want my waters to flow back to me in peace, not filled with pieces of debris."

"What do you mean? Are you saying you're ready to leave us and go to heaven, Granny?"

"Well, we should always be ready. Never know when the good Lord will come for ya'. But that's not what I'm saying.

"I want to live my life so full and without regrets that by the time I do leave here, every one of you will know that I was free. I was free from every care, every worry. Free from every, 'I wish I would have done' because I would have done it. All of it, every last bit."

Ruthie rocked in rhythm with her slow-churning thoughts, the kind of slow churning that makes good ole southern butter and homemade ice cream. Slow, purposeful, meaningful motions, like well-thought-out daydreams.

Chapter Nine

RISE AND SHINE

Cheryl emerged from her daylong slumber just in time for dinner. She slowly made her way down the stairs and into the kitchen, the rich aroma of Ruthie's country fried steak and smothered white potatoes guiding her way.

"There's our sleeping beauty," Ruthie said, glancing over her left shoulder. "How's my eldest child?"

"I'm okay."

"You've been in bed all day. I wasn't sure I'd see you at all for the rest of the evening. Are you hungry?"

"Not really. I took a few bites off the sandwich. I just don't have much of an appetite right now."

"Understandable."

"Hi, Mama," Yvonne whispered, lingering at the kitchen door. Her hands rested at her sides, now afraid to embrace the frailty of her mother. She stood on guard and at attention, waiting for her mother's response.

"Hi, Baby."

"Are you all right?"

"I will be. I will be."

"How'd you sleep?" Ruthie asked.

"I slept fine. Can't say I rested much, though. I still feel tired inside. I probably could've slept straight through the night, but I don't think I'll ever get enough sleep to push this kinda tired away. I decided to just get up and try again later."

"Well, later won't be much longer. It's almost bedtime now," Ruthie said. "Maybe you should take a nice warm bath. It'll relax you a bit. I can make you some chamomile tea or some warm milk."

"Tea is fine."

The sound of clanking keys echoed through the front screen door. Sheila had arrived just in time for dinner. Entering the Boyd abode, she checked a small stack of mail set atop the floor-model Zenith TV. While the sheer pink curtains blew lightly through the open windows, she made quiet, purposeful steps across the worn beige carpet, as if instinctively knowing the previous tone of the home. Sheila set down her bag, partly filled with Sheba hosiery, on the living room floor. She then exchanged a warm smile with Yvonne, now seated at the dining room table and carefully peeling green apples for Ruthie's fried dessert pies.

Meanwhile, conversation flowed freely but almost superficially between Cheryl and Ruthie—neither yet ready to acknowledge the true meaning behind their words. Hurt laid hidden beneath the surface of their discourse about as well as black lace underneath a white veil.

"I'm okay with letting go now, Mama. I'm not sure when it happened, but I'm okay now. It doesn't mean I've given up on things ever getting better. I think I've just come to terms with things never being the same, or at least not what I originally expected, you know?" Cheryl said. "If he comes back to me again whole and well, then so be it. And if he doesn't, then so be that, too. Either way it goes, it won't be the same as it was before. I won't let it. *I* won't be the same. Too much has happened, and it's changed me. Hurts like the ones Jimmy put me through change a woman, maybe even for the better. You can't help that.

"No matter how much you hold onto the anchor of hope, the winds of change are bound to leave some holes in your sail. But at least I'm still floating. I'm still standing. And for now, that's more than enough."

"Yes, it most certainly is enough," Ruthie concurred. "I couldn't have said it better myself."

"Amen, Sister," Sheila chimed in on Cheryl and Ruthie's conversation. "Now, what are we talking about?"

"Thanks, Mama. That means a lot."

"So, Cheryl, how do you feel?" Ruthie asked.

"I'm disappointed, at best. But as long as I'm still breathing, there's always the chance things could get better, I guess. I'm holding on to that, really tight."

"Child, just because you can barely breathe doesn't mean God didn't give you air. He's still in the supply and demand business. I thank heaven every day that no man has his hand on the sun's on-and-off switch but God. As long as He's still in control, the sun will rise tomorrow just like it did today, and everything will be all right."

"Um . . . what are we talking about?" Sheila said.

"The sun rises and shines new every morning, no matter how dark it got the night before. So to me, if the sun can do it, I can too. I'm just gonna let my little light shine. I figure my job is nowhere near as hard as the sun's."

"I guess that's one way of looking at it," Cheryl said.

"Believe it or not, Cheryl, Mama understands just how you feel. True, I had a different set of circumstances along the way, but they produced the same results—a woman feeling tired and all alone."

"Am I the invisible man here?" Sheila asked again.

"What are you talkin' about, Mama? You're far from alone,"

Cheryl said. "You and Papa been together what, thirty years?"

"No. We've been married thirty years. We haven't been *together* for nearly any of it."

"Wait a minute. What's really going on here?" Sheila insisted. "How can you say that, Mama?"

"The same way you can ask that. Perception is everything. You're on the outside looking in on what you think marriage is supposed to be," Ruthie said. "Well, let me back up a minute. I don't want to assume anything.

"Two questions for you both: What do you think marriage is supposed to look like, and what do you think marriage is supposed to feel like?"

"Man, that's heavy," Cheryl replied. "I'm married, but I'm not sure I know the answer."

"Well, Sheila, what do you say?"

"I don't know what I just walked into," Sheila said, "but, Mama, what you and Papa have is what I think marriage looks like and feels like."

"So what do we have?"

"A loving relationship built on trust and commitment."

"That's what you say, baby girl, but what have you actually seen?"

"Mama, you're scaring me. I've never heard you talk this way about you and Papa." Sheila said. "What are you and Cheryl really talking about, and where did all of this come from in the first place? Things weren't perfect when I left for work this morning, but they weren't this strange."

Ruthie and Cheryl exchanged looks and instinctively made a silent vow never to speak of the day's events to Sheila. She was still too impressionable to handle it one way or the other. Sure, Yvonne may have seen bits and pieces of things, but she was stronger and still young—young enough to forget, young enough to think that what she saw was just her imagination.

"Never you mind, Shay," Ruthie said, nullifying any emphasis on her previous words. "No need troubling yourself with such things. We're just having women's talk, that's all."

"Aren't I a woman, too?" Sheila asked in defiance.

A nod of agreement was the only confirmation Ruthie could muster up for Sheila. Ruthie was already concerned that Sheila spent too much time and energy focused on Bobby. The last thing she needed was to let Jimmy's flaws magnify Bobby's mere potential in Sheila's eyes. Sheila was just too impressionable, with too much to lose. There was no sense in having two daughters on the brink of self-destruction over a man. Ruthie made up her mind right then that if Sheila ever learned of what happened that day, it would not be from her lips, but from Cheryl's very own. Cheryl, no doubt, had already crawled into a cave of shame and determined never to speak of it again.

John walked through the back porch door as if summoned on cue, no doubt a welcome distraction from the unspoken awkwardness of dodging the truth.

"What's happenin', Pops?" John asked rhetorically. Receiving only a partial response from the nodding Papa Boyd, John entered the family kitchen.

"Mmm-mm. Something smells good, Mama," John said, leaning over to kiss Ruthie's cheek. "Man, I got all three Boyd women in the kitchen at the same time. You know what they say about too many chefs. Don't y'all go burning up my dinner with all your gossip."

"Boy, I tell you. You always come in ready to start something," Sheila said.

"You know you wouldn't have me no other way. What y'all ladies into, anyway?"

"Nothing much," Cheryl responded.

"I'm still trying to figure it out," Sheila said. "You know what? Mama just said that she and Papa don't love each other anymore."

"Say what?" John said.

"That's not at all what I said," Ruthie recanted. "If you're going to read between the lines of my newspaper story, at least get the headline right."

"She got you told, Shay," John said.

"What I said was that we've been married thirty years; but we haven't been *together* for nearly any of it."

"I don't see much of a difference between the two statements, Mother," Sheila said.

"But I do," John added. "There are a lot of couples out here who love each other plenty, they just can't get solid. They can't seem to get on the same page, you dig? It's like they love each other, they just can't seem to work together.

"A prime example is Cheryl and Jimmy," John said. "Cheryl's over here moping all day and snapping off on the preacher man because she misses Jimmy. And I just saw Jimmy crying into a beer I bought him at Joe's 'cause he misses Cheryl. They love each other plenty, but for whatever reason, Cheryl just won't take him back."

"There you go meddling again. *For whatever reason?*" Cheryl rebutted. "*Cheryl* won't take him back? What's there to take back, John? Jimmy's a wreck and you know it."

"I didn't say he wasn't. But last time I checked, you didn't look like you just came off the showroom floor yourself. And I don't see *Jet Magazine* beating down your door for beauty of the week either."

"You don't know what you're talking about, John! You don't know—"

"Time out, both of you!" Ruthie shouted, slamming a metal spoon down on the stove. "At what point in your *adult* lives do I get to stop playing referee?

"Cheryl, you just can't keep flying off the handle at folks. And John, you can't keep talking about stuff when you only know half the story. When are you two gonna help each other grow up?"

"Mama, I don't mean no harm. I don't see what the big fuss is between Jimmy and Cheryl, anyway. Why can't they just talk it out? She never said what went wrong. Cheryl, you can tell me. If he did something to hurt you, I'm your brother. Tell me."

"John, you're just as short-fused as Jimmy and you ain't seen one day in Vietnam," Ruthie said. "How is she supposed to feel at ease telling you anything?"

"John, thanks for the offer," Cheryl said, "but you have no idea what's going on. Heck, I can't even make heads or tails of it."

"Well, on another note," Sheila said, trying to divert another argument. "Let me show off this pretty new dress Robert bought me today while I was on my lunch break." Sheila had retrieved her plastic Montgomery Ward bag and was rummaging through its contents.

In sync with the sound of a rattling bag, Yvonne turned her head to see the latest addition to her Auntie Shay's collection of trinkets.

"Oh, here it is. Isn't it lovely?" Sheila said, beaming.

Sheila pulled out her brand-new sundress, red with white polka dots, compliments of Mr. Robert Johnston.

Yvonne dropped her paring knife to the floor.

CALM BEFORE THE STORM

Dinner now complete, Cheryl cradled her promised cup of chamomile tea and elected to retire early for the evening. Sheila, in contrast, headed out for a late movie date with Bobby while John retreated to the basement for his own spot of solitude.

Yvonne carefully gathered two mason jars from the cupboard, steadily pouring fresh lemonade as Ruthie supervised her new chore.

Hearing cabinets open and then close, Papa Boyd stirred from dozing in his worn brown recliner long enough to call out, "Who's there?"

"Who do you think?"

With her robotic response given, Ruthie nodded to signal Yvonne out of the house and toward the front porch. The two assumed their positions in Ms. Pittman's old cedars. Yvonne rocked a little harder this evening, hoping to drown out the deafening noise of the big people now churning around in her own head.

"Everything all right, Grandbaby? You seem a little preoccupied tonight."

"Oh, I'm fine, Granny. Just thinking about Mama, that's all."

"Never you mind about your Mama. The good Lord knows how to take better care of her than you and me put together. Besides, I think she's more clearheaded today than she's been in a long time."

"I guess so. I wonder if I should even go upstairs to sleep tonight. I don't want to be in her way. I feel like I'm in the way."

"You're no bother to your Mama, child. It might be a good idea for you to stay downstairs tonight, though—on account of the heat, that's all. It's too hot upstairs anyway and I don't want you to get heat bumps. I'll lay out a pallet for you in the front room. That way you can even stay up and watch a little late-night TV with me."

"Can I watch Johnny Carson?"

"I think we can work that out. Our secret, though."

"I won't tell a soul. Granny?"

"Yes, Vonnie?"

"What do you think of Auntie Shay's new dress? It's pretty, isn't it? I saw a lady today wearing the same dress. She was pretty, too. Well, kind of."

"Grandbaby, don't go getting fixated on pretty dresses and pretty people. There's often a bit of ugly in the prettiest of people."

"Whatcha mean by that, Granny?"

"What I mean is that everyone has a little part of them that's not picture-perfect or pretty-fine all the time. We all can have some ways that aren't so pleasing, especially the pretty people."

"Pretty people, Granny?"

"Yes, the pretty people. That's what I call the ones who walk around like they've got it all together and all figured out, and even the ones who seem too good to be true."

"I might know some pretty people myself, since you put it that way."

"Grandbaby, remember that. Don't ever be so impressed by those who always got their pants creased tight and their hem straight, 'cause they've got problems too. They might even have some secrets. Heck, the song says beauty's only skin deep but ugly's to the bone!"

"You betcha. Then I think men can be pretty people, too."

"Sure, they can. The Lord's no respecter of persons. What's good for the goose is good for the gander, too."

"I know that's right, 'cause today I saw Bob—" Yvonne said with a sudden halt, choosing instead to swallow another dose of big people's problems.

"You saw who?"

"I saw, um—um—I saw—I forgot what I was about to say."

"That's too funny. Maybe you're more like me than I realized. Looks like my old age is catching up with *you*. Maybe we should go in early tonight. Besides, we have to get ready for 'Here's Johnny!'"

Yvonne laughed instinctively rather than taking the chance of saying anything else that would expose Sheila's situation. Wise beyond her years, Yvonne knew she was often Sheila's only advocate in the Boyd home. Sharing the unfortunate news with Ruthie first would leave Sheila wide open and unprepared for a barrage of I-told-you-sos. That would have been unfair, not to mention an outright betrayal of their friendship. Yvonne convinced herself that if anyone should know what she saw, it should first be Sheila.

Yvonne thought it best to give Sheila time to prepare her rebuttal to Ruthie's certain onslaught of interrogation and debate. The question, however, was how she could tell Sheila, or whether it was even her place to tell at all. Her previously clear plumb line between childhood and pubescence had grown more blurred with each forward motion of the cedar chair. Hoping to hold on to one more night of definitive innocence, Yvonne quickly followed Ruthie inside for a numbing dose of comedy and a summertime treat of a pallet on the living room floor.

* * *

The next morning, Yvonne's sleep was stirred by a clicking noise at the front door. It was Sheila, and once again 7:00 a.m.

"Auntie Shay?" Yvonne asked, her voice still groggy.

"Yes, it's me," she whispered. "Go back to sleep or you'll wake your Granny."

"Too late," Ruthie said, standing at her bedroom doorway, tying a knot in her housecoat belt. "I heard you fumbling with your keys."

"Mama!"

"Yes, it's me. And maybe you should finally go to bed. Or have you already done that elsewhere?"

"Mama?"

"Don't Mama me! All this talk about respect and love, and this is what you lower yourself to do? Where are your standards? And where's the respect for my house?"

"There you go assuming things again, Mama. For Christ's sake, you don't know everything!"

"First of all, don't you ever raise your voice at me again! I don't care how old you are. Second of all, don't you ever use the Lord's name in vain in my house! You better lower your voice before you wake up your Papa and the whole neighborhood. Oh, but I forgot: the people on the block probably know more about your whereabouts last night than I do."

Ruthie turned her back and stomped to the kitchen, slamming the cast iron coffee pot onto the stove. Sheila took the gesture as a sign of disrespect and ignorantly followed Ruthie to stand her ground.

"You don't know everything, Mama!"

"No, Sheila. *You* don't know everything!" Ruthie shouted, now pointing in Sheila's defiant face. "You're only eighteen, Shay. You get your first man and think you're automatically a woman. You don't know what this fella is all about or who he's even been with, Sheila. What kind of respectable man makes you sneak out of your parents' home—the same parents he hasn't had the decency to even meet? Why hasn't he joined us for a Sunday dinner if he's so honorable?

"You've been sneaking around with him nearly six months. He never comes in the house when he picks you up. He only honks the car horn or, on a good day, stands at the door, but he never comes in the house. What's that all about, Sheila?"

"You make him sound like he's using me. He's not like that, Mama! And besides, it wasn't long after my age that you were already married with children!"

"Things were different back then, and you don't know all of what I went through being married with children that young."

"Well, Bobby's not like that and I'm tired of always having to defend him."

"Baby, a real man won't put you in a position to have to defend him. He'll be defending you."

"I'm done with it! I'm grown and I can do what I want!" Sheila said, turning to walk away.

"Well I hope he has a home for you to go to since you can't seem to respect mine!"

Half asleep, half in shock, Yvonne stood yet again at the kitchen door—her usual front-row seat to the Boyd women's drama. Sheila stomped right by her without even a glance and ran to her bedroom. Her door slam could be heard throughout the entire house. Ruthie returned the gesture, slamming cabinet doors after retrieving the sugar, then cream. The exchange of noise permeated throughout the walls as if two dark clouds had clashed in a clap of thunder.

It was ten o'clock before another Boyd was bold enough to emerge. Cheryl, feeling more like herself and selectively oblivious to the prior commotion, checked to see whether Yvonne had washed, dressed, and eaten. All had been overseen compliments of Ruthie, who welcomed the distraction of caregiving from the early morning clamor.

Ruthie herself, now dressed, announced with a hint of defiance, "I'm taking a walk!"

She decided to take an impromptu break from her routine of one walk to the park per week. Ruthie was in need of an emergency dose of peace.

As she strutted down the familiar concrete path, she felt anticipation building within her. They were waiting for her. At least they still embraced her. Who? Her memories.

* * *

Club DeLisa was barely lit that crisp Friday night in March 1941. The dance hall was accented by art deco wall sconces. Tealight candles adorned the snugly spaced tabletops. A melodious clamor of trumpets and snare drums vibrated the rustic floorboards. The faint smell of whiskey, intensified by body heat, cigarette smoke, and Chantilly Lace, filled the air—yet no one seemed to mind.

This particular night, Ruthie sat facing the door, sipping occasionally on a cold root beer. She hadn't seen Monroe Jackson since they met on New Year's Eve, but heard he might be there. After all, Club DeLisa was the place to be for a Friday night jazz set on State Street. If not there, the 708 Club on Forty-Seventh Street was the spot for live blues from the likes of Muddy Waters or Howlin' Wolf. Club DeLisa, however, was all the rage with its swing dancing, jitter bugging, and the best headliners, from Cab Calloway to Joe Williams. People were about as excited to get there as some were for church on Sunday morning. This night was no different.

The house band was up first. As if in sync with the rhythm of

Ruthie's heart, in walked Monroe, two songs into the set. Ruthie's second impression of him was the same as her first: he was just like a good cup of coffee—tall, dark, and warm. They'd hit it off right away when they met before, like they had known each other all the time. Now she wondered if the chemistry was still there or if Monroe had forgotten all about her.

"Girl, he's here," Ruthie exclaimed to Earnestine.

"Where, Ruthie?"

"Right there, in the gray pinstriped suit. Isn't he a looker?"

"Mmm-hmm. Now, girl, that's what I'm saying. He's handsome and a sharp dresser, too. Must mean he already has a good job lined up."

"He's on his way to the service. Navy, I think. Oh, goodness. I think he just saw me, Earnestine."

"Well, wave at him."

"I'm too nervous."

"Forget you. I'll do it." Earnestine stood in her chair and shouted out his name, "Monroe!"

Looking up, Monroe spotted the boy-crazed Earnestine waving frantically in his direction. Then he saw her point to Ruthie, too. Without hesitation, Monroe made his way through the crowd to take the final open seat at their table.

"Some set of pipes you've got there. I heard you clear across the room, even with all this noise."

"What can I say? Those years of cheerleading finally paid off," Earnestine said. "You remember my best friend Ruthie, don't ya? She was at Tommy's New Year's Eve party."

"How could I forget? We talked and danced the whole night. How are you, Ruthie?"

"Just peachy," Ruthie said, trying to speak with an even tone over her racing heartbeat. "I haven't seen you around in a while."

"Yeah, I know. I've been working a few extra shifts down at the stockyards. I just wanted to save up a little cash for my Mom and Pop to have while I'm away."

"Where are you going?"

"I'm still off to the navy. It won't be until the fall now, but I still want to get things in order before I ship off to basic training."

"All this talk about work and boats is a bit boring to me," Earnestine interjected, winking at Ruthie. "I think I'll go to the ladies' room and then sit closer to the stage for a while."

"Well, I don't think it's boring at all, Monroe," Ruthie said.

"You don't have to be nice. I can get a little talkative sometimes," Monroe said. "What about you? What have you been into lately?"

That was the first time a guy had ever asked Ruthie that question and really meant it.

"Me? Oh, I'm in my senior year and taking advanced sewing classes at school. I really want to be a seamstress. I have a dream that maybe I'll even design my own prom dress. Who knows?"

"You're a smart cookie. I'm sure you can do anything you set your mind to do," Monroe said, smiling at Ruthie with his eyes. "So who's taking you to your prom?"

"Oh, I don't know. It's a few months from now. Earnestine already knows Tommy's taking her. As for me, who knows?"

"How about me? I could take you. That is, if you wanted me to."

"You? You hardly know me."

"This is March. Prom's in May, right? I figure that gives me until then to get to know you plenty. So what do ya say?"

"It's just so sudden, but . . . I'd like that very much."

* * *

Monroe kept his promise of getting to know Ruthie in the few months leading up to her senior prom. He was as smitten with Ruthie as she had been with him. Their budding courtship was inevitable.

Monroe didn't have a car of his own yet, but made it his business to borrow his father's old Ford whenever he could. When the hooptie wasn't available, Monroe made his weekly pilgrimage to visit his beloved Ruthie. He rode two different streetcars to pick Ruthie up after her church service, and then the two rode those same streetcars back to his house for Sunday dinner. He often bragged to Ruthie about his mother's cooking and said his future wife had to learn from the best. The two lovebirds spent every Sunday evening watching the *Ed Sullivan Show* in the Jacksons' family room, Monroe's head resting in Ruthie's lap.

Ruthie was always self-conscious about Monroe's open affection, but he never held back. He loved being with her, and she loved being with him. Those moments were precious to them both, engraved in the memories of their hearts forever. Their connection was constant and easy. They were friends, companions, dreamers.

Raised as a true Southern gentleman, Monroe personally escorted Ruthie back home on that same two-streetcar commute each and every time. He then took the last two of his eight streetcar rides back home. He was falling in love, and so was she.

Monroe escorted Ruthie to her prom as he had promised. Ruthie designed and sewed her own pearl-white chiffon gown, just as she had dreamed. That summer the two were inseparable, spending every free moment together. Ruthie got her first job as a seamstress at Pride Dry Cleaners on Seventy-Ninth Street. Monroe was still working to save up money for his folks to use while he was away. Monroe and Ruthie talked constantly about what they wanted out of life and how they could make all of their dreams come true.

The once-vibrant green leaves were now signaling the inevitability of fall. It was time for Monroe to report for basic training. Ruthie had known the day would come, yet nothing could soothe the pangs in her heart.

"Don't worry, Ruthie," Monroe reassured her. "I promise to make you my wife when my tour of duty is over. Three years will go by so quick, your head will spin."

Monroe, forever the planner, figured the time apart would be productive for them both, giving Ruthie a chance to take up classes at the city college and allowing him time to save for their future. To Ruthie, however, three years away seemed an unbearable eternity.

After completing boot camp and an advanced training stint in Detroit, Monroe made a surprise visit home before being shipped off two weeks later for good. Their love had grown even more. Monroe even gave Ruthie his mother's engagement ring as a sign of his commitment.

A night parked on lovers' lane before his deployment seemed right. It was a natural progression of their love. It was everything they'd both wanted, yet it changed everything in the way only life can.

* * *

Monroe was on active duty, floating on some sea, when Ruthie discovered she was pregnant. Her family would consider her grown enough for a baby at nineteen, but few would embrace a church-going, disgraced, unwed mother. She should have known better, people would say.

She was too old to be shipped off down South to unfamiliar relatives to have her child in shame. What would become of her now? What should she do? Ruthie wondered whether to tell Monroe at all, out of fear that the stress of another mouth to feed would put him in harm's way. Nevertheless she chose to break the news to him in a letter. Ruthie decided to be direct, stating her premise bluntly in the first few lines she wrote: "Monroe, I have something to tell you that may not be easy to hear. I'm pregnant. I'm scared, but I love you. I hope you still want to marry me."

Scared was an understatement. Fear so gripped Ruthie that she panicked and began to question everything Monroe had ever promised her, and with good reason. Even though she soon received an anxious yet jovial letter in response from Monroe, she never told him that she lived in a home with an abusive father whom she feared. As far as Monroe knew, Ruthie and their unborn child would be perfectly safe until he returned. He would do his part financially as well as he could until they were reunited as a family. However, Ruthie lived with a time bomb, and every memory of freedom she'd experienced with Monroe pushed her closer to the brink of desperation. She couldn't live there another moment more, let alone raise a child there. It would be years before Monroe was finished with the navy.

Ruthie felt trapped, pressured to act fast, and sought out her best friend for a listening ear.

"Hi, Ruthie! Come on in," Earnestine said, opening the door to her parents' home.

Stepping across the threshold, Ruthie immediately burst into tears.

"What's the matter, girl? Sit down. You're a mess."

"I'm—I'm—I'm pregnant. I don't know what to do."

"Oh, no! Have you told Monroe?"

"Yes, I wrote him a letter and he wrote me back right away."

"So, what did he say?"

"He said not to worry about anything. That he loves me and we're still getting married. In his eyes, we just started our family first."

"Good. He's always been a gentleman to you. I knew he'd do the right thing. So why are you crying so hard? Are your parents giving you a hard time about it?"

"I haven't even told them about the baby yet. Besides, I never told you this. I've never told anyone, not even Monroe, but my father beats us. He has for years," Ruthie muttered through sobs. "It's been so bad that one time my brother had to go to the emergency room for a broken arm. We told everyone he fell climbing a tree. I'm scared to tell him. I'm so scared."

"Are you serious? But he's a deacon. He's the first one in church every Sunday, and the last one to leave!"

"I know. That's why I've never said anything. It would be such an embarrassment to the whole family if anyone ever knew."

"Well, you don't have anything to worry about now. I won't tell a soul, and you're about to marry Mr. Wonderful. You can live happily ever after."

"I know, but I can't live like this for another three years, especially with a baby. I can't put my baby in danger, too. And once my mother finds out, she's going to say, 'You're full grown now. It's time for you to stand on your own.' I only make seven dollars a week at the dry cleaner's. How can I support a baby on my own for three years on that kind of money?"

"You don't have to. Just tell Monroe. Maybe you can even stay with his mom until he comes home for good."

"I can't do that. I don't think his mother even likes me, and once she finds this out, she'll never like me. I feel like I'm trapped in a dream that went all wrong. If I tell Monroe everything, maybe he won't see me as the same smart person. Maybe he won't love me the same. I don't want him being with me out of pity. And the money he's saved up over the last year is for his parents. He's always said that. Who am I to try to stand in the way of him and his folks?"

"You're the mother of his unborn child, that's who you are! Say something to him, or I will!"

"No, Earnestine. Promise me you won't," Ruthie pleaded through her tears. "I have to figure this out by myself. Don't tell him. If I can't have his love the same way that I've experienced it so far, I'd rather live without it. I feel ashamed when I talk about what I've experienced with my father. I don't want to ever feel that way when I'm with Monroe."

"That's my friend, Ms. Truthie Ruthie. Only thing is, this time around, what you're standing true to isn't true at all. It's just the way you perceive things to be. You've got too much pride to ask Monroe for help, and you're too down on yourself to receive love. What a combination!"

"Promise me, Earnestine. Promise me."

"Okay. I promise."

* * *

Over the next year, Ruthie had her firstborn child, a girl she named Cheryl Tucker. As she expected, tensions rose in her parents' home over the extra mouth to feed and she felt the pressure to leave. Her correspondence with Monroe had turned shallow at best—her doing. She was slowly withdrawing from him, from the dream she now thought was out of her reach.

Ruthie took her baby and moved into a small kitchenette with three roommates, Betty-Joe Harper, Joanne Jacobs, and Marie-Lou Bell. The women paired up in the sleeping quarters and shared the small kitchen and bathroom down the hall. There were five children between them.

Times were hard for Ruthie, and she struggled to stretch the seven dollars to cover room and board, diapers and milk, and babysitting fees. Part of her was still counting the days until Monroe's return, but with each strenuous moment came the reminder that she was gasping for air.

One Sunday in church, Ruthie was approached by a young man who knew she had an arm baby but was willing to court her anyway.

Still living her life in panic mode, Ruthie accepted his invitation to dinner. Her heart was really miles away, but she had a child to feed. She was scared senseless and tired of feeling all alone.

Ruthie's fears ran a marathon through her mind. What if Monroe reenlisted? What if he got killed in the line of duty and never made it home? What if someone else had caught his eye? What if this new suitor was her only chance at more in life? What if no one else would have her as a wife with another man's child? With all these questions harassing her into senseless reaction, Ruthie took the opportunity for a here-and-now kind of love. She needed a provider, and this man needed a supporter. They began a courtship of mutual admiration, but knowingly absent of true love.

"I don't love you, but I can grow to love you," she once said.

The two married in a small unassuming ceremony just six months later. No church. Only a small cake and a few friends. Ruthie wore black, as if mourning the loss of one life for another. Monroe only learned of Ruthie's nuptials in a telegram sent to him one year later by Tommy. He thought Monroe should know before embarrassing himself when he came back home.

Monroe had continued to write Ruthie, but his letters to her parents' address had gone unanswered. When he got back home, he desperately tried to find her or to get a message to her through mutual friends. Nothing came of it. Ruthie had already signed on the dotted line of marriage and was committed to leaving the past behind. The lovebirds were no more.

Her name became Ruthie Boyd. Her husband inconspicuously raised Cheryl as his own, last name and all. Yet through the years, the terms of agreement that were once good enough for her and Papa Boyd had lost their validity. The words, "I don't love you, but I can grow to love you," had drifted from being a hope for more to a disdain for not enough. One day they both looked up and realized that love, true love, would have been worth the wait, but they resolved that their contract was legally binding.

"Ice cream. Ice cream. Ma'am, would you care for some ice cream? Ma'am. Ma'am?"

"Oh, I'm sorry, baby. You have to forgive me. I guess I'm getting to be an old lady. Just got a little too carried away daydreaming. What did you ask me again?"

"I'm selling ice cream out my buggy here. I saw you sitting out here in the park on this beautiful sunny day and thought you might like some."

"You know, that might not be such a bad idea. I could eat it before I got home to my grandbaby. She'd have no part of me walking in that house without one in my hand for her. I'll have one ice cream sandwich, please."

"Yes, ma'am. That will be fifty cents."

"Then fifty cents it is. Here you go, son."

"Thanks, ma'am. Maybe you should move to a bench in the shade."

"You're probably right. I think I've had enough sunlight and revelation for one day."

Chapter Eleven

TRUTH OR DARE

Dear Diary,

> *I love summertime.*
> *Flip-flops clapping under feet.*
> *Green trees in the breeze.*

I like poems. They make me happy. I guess I just needed something to make me happy because I'm about to burst holding in this secret. What secret, you ask? The one about Auntie Sheila's boyfriend Bobby. Thelma and I saw him outside the laundromat last week. He was loading his car with a lot of clean clothes. Too many for one person. Then I saw a lady come out. She kissed him on the lips and then got into his car.

Granny and Auntie Shay got into a big argument a few days ago because she stayed out all night with Bobby. I've wanted to tell Sheila about Mr. Bobby so bad, but she's been too angry. Granny's been angry, too. I'm trying not to choose sides, but it's hard because I know the truth. I just don't get why big people play pretend more than kids do. Auntie Shay's pretending like Bobby's good to her. Mama's pretending that she's okay. Granny's pretending that I don't see things that are right in front of me, and she keeps taking long walks to clear her head. I wish they would just grow up and talk. But I'm just a kid. What do I know?

Until next time.

Love,
Yvonne

The days since Ruthie and Sheila's brawl had a stale feeling in the air. All the Boyds could sense it, as if the exhale of combative words had produced a toxic residue that shouldn't be inhaled. The others instead chose the temporary solace of an unspoken safety zone on a nearly palpable emotional battlefield. Cheryl was no different in that matter. She had enough of her own issues to figure out.

Cheryl had not worked consistently in the past three months. The stress of things with Jimmy had proven to be more than she could endure. She broke down in tears one day while checking out a shopper at the Jewel, where she had worked for five years. The manager told her to take some time off, that her job would be there when she was ready to come back.

Life was coming at Cheryl hard despite her lack of preparation for it. Ready or not, here life came, day after day, heartache after heartache. She knew she had to pull herself back together, especially the pieces that had been shattered by Jimmy's latest emotional grenade. She still wasn't ready to tell it all. Somehow putting it into words made it more real than the night it happened. Yet she had to start making her way back to life, back to her purpose—the greatest of which at this point was being a mother to Yvonne.

"So what are you into today, Little Mama?" Cheryl asked Yvonne, who was stretched out belly down and ankles crossed on the living room floor.

"Poetry, that's all."

"Poetry? I didn't know you liked to write poems," Cheryl said, turning the TV on to *Days of Our Lives*.

"I didn't know either until I got the diary from Auntie Shay."

"Hmm. So I see you're getting well acquainted with your personal thoughts, there."

"Yeah, it's nice to be able to talk about things."

"You know you can talk to me, right?"

"Yeah, I guess. I just don't want to be in the way."

"Baby, you're never in the way. I know I haven't been myself lately. I've been through a lot; we both have been. I guess it's just taken more of a toll on me than I realized. I hope you can forgive me for some of my recent outbursts. I guess I just couldn't hold it in anymore."

"I know it's hard trying to be big all the time, Mama."

"You've got that right. I guess that's why I was so resistant to you getting a diary in the first place. Seems to me that diaries just encourage you to have secrets, and the more secrets you keep, the more of an adult you become."

"That sounds strange to me, Mama. I thought adults were the ones who knew to always tell the truth?"

"Baby, knowing to do something and actually doing it are two totally different things. A lot of 'big people,' as you call us, know the right thing to do, but that doesn't mean we always get it right."

"Mama, can I tell you something?"

"Sure. You can tell me anything."

"If I tell you, you have to promise not to say anything because someone might get hurt."

"Someone? Someone like who?"

"Um . . . um, maybe I shouldn't say anything."

"So you're becoming like us big people after all?"

"No, Mama. I just don't want things to get worse, that's all. And if I tell you my secret, they just might."

"Okay, then. What if I promise not to tell unless you say it's okay? Will that help?"

"I guess so. I just don't want anyone to get hurt. I'm just not sure which would be more hurtful, for the person to know what I know, or to be left in the dark about the whole thing?"

"Wait a minute. This sounds pretty serious. Tell me what you know. I still promise not to say anything unless you say it's okay. It just sounds like this particular secret may be a bit much for even a soon-to-be thirteen-year-old to handle alone."

"Well, okay then. Mama, I saw Bobby."

"Bobby? Sheila's Bobby?"

"Yes."

"Okay, Secret Squirrel. Can you give me a little more to go on than that? You saw Bobby where, doing what?"

"I was walking to the candy store with Thelma and we saw him loading up his car with a lot of laundry."

"Sweetheart, that sounds pretty normal to me."

"No, Mama, a lot of laundry. It was too much laundry for one person alone. Then when I called his name to say hi, he ignored me. That's when I saw her come out to the car."

"You saw who?"

"I think he has another girlfriend because he kissed her on the mouth. Then he rushed in the car, did a U-turn and sped away."

"What? You saw him kissing someone else, Yvonne? Are you serious?"

"Yes. Plus she was wearing the same dress Bobby just gave Auntie Sheila."

"Oh . . . my . . . goodness. When did this happen?"

"It's been about a week ago now. So much was going on so I didn't know who I could tell. No one knows but me and Thelma, and she promised not to tell. Please don't say anything to Auntie,

Mama. She's so happy and I don't want to be the one to hurt her."

"Sweetheart, you have nothing to do with hurting her. Bobby has taken care of that all by himself.

"Oh, my goodness. Okay. Don't worry about anything. I'll handle it."

"What are you going to do, Mama?"

"I don't know just yet, Yvonne. I have to think about it. Things may just work themselves out. Sometimes secrets need to be exposed. Other times they tend to rise to the top on their own. The Good Book says that a little leaven leavens the whole loaf. Well, let's just say that this secret has enough leaven in it to raise a whole loaf of Wonder Bread, baby.

"Like I said, don't worry about it. I'll handle it. You just concentrate on something more suitable for your mind to handle. How about you come up with a list of how you want to celebrate your birthday next Sunday, and I'll see what parts I can actually make happen for you."

"Thanks, Mama. And thanks for keeping my secret."

"You're welcome. I can't make any promises on how things will work out with Shay, but I can say that I won't betray your trust. I'll keep you in the know."

"Talk about keeping folks in the know—look what I just found in the basement," John said, slipping in on the tail end and making a rare daytime appearance.

"Thanks for just barging in on our girl talk, Baby Brother," Cheryl said.

"Sho you right. I aim to please," John said. "Look at this stuff. I found this old crate filled with all these pictures of Mama. They must be from when she was in high school."

"Oh, wow! Let me see!" Yvonne said, now perched on her knees.

"Yeah, I was looking to see if I could find any of Papa's old blues records and I stumbled across this crate. Let's see what else is in here," John said, rummaging through the archives of Ruthie's memories. "Here's Mama's high school diploma. Valedictorian! She never told us that she was that smart."

"Wow. Granny was valedictorian of her class?"

"It appears so," Cheryl said, handling the documents with care.

"Let's see what else is in this treasure box," John continued. "Hmm, there's a picture here of a man in a naval uniform. I wonder who this is because Papa was in the army. Here the guy is again in another picture, hugged up with Mama. It's dated 1942."

"That's strange. I was born in 1942," Cheryl said. "Plus Mama and Papa got married in late 1942, right? The date must be wrong, John. Look again."

"Mama, how could you be born the same year they got married?"

"It's possible, Yvonne. There are twelve months in a year, but it only takes nine of them to make a baby."

"Sis, there are a few letters here, too. They're all from an M. Jackson based in Michigan and stationed overseas. The postmark on some of them is from 1941 to 1943."

"Well, open them up."

John opened a letter, glanced at the first two sentences, and immediately returned it to its time-stained envelope.

"Why are you putting that away, John? You've got my curiosity piqued now," Cheryl said. "I want to know more about this M. Jackson character."

"You know what? We're sitting here, going through Mama's personal things without her permission. I'm not getting into trouble for you."

"Getting in trouble for me? You sound like we're still kids. Besides, you're the one who brought the box up here in the first place."

"Yeah, and I just remembered I've got to go anyway. There's a meeting down at the NAACP office that I need to be at in thirty minutes."

"What? Well, leave the box with me and I'll take it back down to the basement later."

"Now I know for a fact that you're nosy, Sis. You know good and well you don't like going in the basement to do your laundry, let alone snoop through cobweb-covered boxes."

"I guess you know me pretty well," Cheryl said with a chuckle. "I guess this mystery romance of Mama's is to be continued. Ms. Yvonne, this is between us. I'll keep your secret and you keep mine. Capisce?"

"Capisce."

"Oh, man. Yvonne, you better watch out. Your Mama just went all Italian Mafia on you. And I thought you didn't like *The Godfather*, Cheryl," John said jokingly, neatly placing all the items back inside the crate. "Okay, ladies, I'm off to the meeting. Tell Mama I may be back in time for dinner."

"Okay, Little Brother, but don't think I won't bring this up again."

"Of course you will, Cheryl. Of course you will."

John now gone, Cheryl diverted her attention back to the TV screen. Somehow her personal drama always seemed to pale in comparison to Doug and Julie's scripted dilemmas. Now, with Sheila's situation brewing in her thoughts, there was something else to take the mental magnifying glass away from her own pain. Her little sister was in trouble and needed her, but how could she help someone as headstrong and stubborn as Shay? Defiance may as well have been Sheila's middle name. She had always been strong-willed. It was that same tenacious spirit that made her an honor roll student at the head of her class. Yet this time, that rebellion may have come back to bite her. Cheryl had just promised Yvonne that she would think of a way to help Sheila without hurting her. How in the world could she do both at the same time?

Soap opera now finished, Cheryl and Yvonne headed to the kitchen for bologna sandwiches and Jay's potato chips. Cheryl stepped in for Ruthie, who had yet to return home, by preparing lunch for Papa Boyd as well. She took his plate to the back porch and placed it on a TV tray, having only small talk about the latest episode of *The Big Valley* before joining Yvonne at the dining room table.

"Boy, that Marie on *Days of Our Lives* gets me every time. I just don't know how one person can be so weak and gullible all at the same time."

"Mama, why are you always watching that show so much if you don't like the actors?"

"What's it to you, Lil' Miss Yvonne?"

"It's just that the soap opera is like Auntie Sheila's life, with all the ups and downs and to-be-continued plots."

"You should watch yourself. You'll be big one day, too. All the right answers might not come so easily to you then. Remember that."

"That sounds like wise advice," Ruthie said, catching the last of their conversation as she walked through the front door.

"Her mouth is as smart as yours was at that age, and Sheila's too," Ruthie interrupted lightheartedly. "I always told you one day you'd have a daughter just like you were at that age, and look-a here."

"Thanks a lot, Mom. I guess now you're a prophet."

"No, I just speak the truth. That's what they used to call me back in high school, you know: Truthie Ruthie. Well, anyway, I'll go unthaw some chicken for tonight. I think I've got a taste for fried chicken, biscuits, and syrup."

"Sounds good, Mama," Cheryl said.

"Did your brother mention whether he'd be home for dinner tonight?"

"He said to tell you that he might."

"Well, that's about as close to a yes as I'll get out of him. He's quite the free spirit, you know."

"Yeah, seems he got it honest," Cheryl said.

"Well, he definitely didn't get a free spirit from his Papa. That man's chained to his chair. As for me being the possible source of freedom? Huh. I stopped feeling that free years before he was ever born."

"If you say so, Mama," Cheryl said, smiling inside. "If you say so."

Chapter Twelve

HE LOVES ME,
HE LOVES ME NOT

Another Sunday morning had dawned in the Boyd household. Sheila chose to cover a friend's shift at work, and Cheryl opted for a brief sabbatical rather than revisit the embarrassment of last Sunday's debacle. That left Ruthie and Yvonne to go to the Lord's house alone.

The eldest and youngest Boyd women exited the house, Yvonne adorned in a yellow gingham sundress with a white cap-sleeved sweater and Ruthie crowned in her white pillbox hat, matching gloves, and a navy-blue dress with three-quarter-length sleeves.

John played his usual role as chauffeur, counting that act within itself as *going* to church. On the Sundays when he actually did enter the building, it was just in time for the sermon. No different than his norm, considering that the only time he was seen at home was just in time for bed, and if he didn't have other plans, he arrived just in time to eat. John's philosophy was to get there—anywhere—for the most important part, whatever the most important part may be. He lived his whole life that way. He had always been a young man of few words, yet observant. He walked tall, as if he alone knew certain things, yet quietly, like he hoped no one would ever make him tell. He dropped Ruthie and Yvonne off, and the two disappeared behind the double doors of Bethesda Church.

John had pulled away slowly, having no particular place to be on a Sunday morning, when he spotted a familiar silhouette a couple of blocks down. It was Jimmy. He was dazed and walking aimlessly down the street in his old fatigues jacket and a pair of holey jeans. John felt sorry for his brother-in-law. He remembered how close they had been before Jimmy enlisted in the service. He remembered hanging out at the jazz club together after Jimmy's sets, and how they laughed and compared notes on some of the silly things Cheryl did or said. He remembered how proud Jimmy was the day Yvonne was born and how he wanted nothing but the best for his little girl. John remembered how much Jimmy had loved his family, and could almost see the cloak of despair on him because of all he had lost in the war.

A lot of people had written Jimmy off, but John's heart went out to him and the other vets who lost their souls in pursuit of honor in a uniform. John knew it would have been easier for people to have compassion on Jimmy if he carried his wounds on the outside. An amputated limb, a wheelchair, or even blinded eyes would have been acceptable to most; but who could respect a man who seemed to have simply come home crazy? John could, and in his own way he tried to extend a lifeline to Jimmy, hoping that one day he could grab ahold of it and finally make his way back home—all the way home.

"What's happening, bro?" John shouted to Jimmy from his now parked car. "Where you headed to, man?"

"Who's that?"

"It's me, man—John."

"Man, that's you?"

"Yeah, jive turkey. Get in. I'll take you to grab some breakfast."

"That sounds out of sight, man. I haven't had a full meal in days," Jimmy said, sliding into John's silver El Dorado.

"So, what you got a taste for, Jimmy?" John said, slowly pulling into traffic.

"Whatever you wanna pay for, that's what my taste buds want."

"You still got that sense of humor," John said. "So how ya been since I saw you last? I mean, really, where do you sleep at night?"

"I'm about the same. I tried to sign up for the VA housing, but the waiting list is three months long. So I stay over at the YMCA when I can get an open slot. They give you one hot meal, a cot, a chance to shower, and then send you on your way. Some days when I can't get a bed there, I just cop a squat underneath the overpass by the Stevenson Expressway. Funny thing is, I've got family who stay right over that way in Le Claire Courts, but they won't let me step foot in the house."

"That's messed up, man."

"Yeah, who you tellin'? It's like they're all scared of me. But I guess I can't blame them 'cause sometimes I scare myself."

"Why?"

"It's like my brain is on automatic rewind. I keep playing the same record over and over, and can't get it to stop."

"Why do you think it's like that?"

"You wouldn't believe some of the stuff I saw over there in 'Nam, man—grenades going off, limbs flying through the air. This one time a guy in my battalion caught a landmine just ten feet in front of me. There was nothing left of him to even send back home to his family, man. Boy, that messed me up something good, because I knew the cat. We'd been through basic training together and everything. Then to see him blown to pieces right in front of me—what do you do with that type of imprint in your brain?

"I was all right for a good while, or at least I thought I was. I guess I was just doing my job. But somehow things got off track when I got back. I just can't seem to get things back on track."

Now at the local pancake house, the two hopped out of the car, entered the restaurant, and grabbed seats at the counter.

"May I take your order?"

"Yeah, give us two of your egg platter specials, two coffees, and a corned beef sandwich. Make the sandwich to go," John said.

"So are you talking to somebody, man?" John asked Jimmy, continuing their conversation from the car. "Did the service give you some medical care or benefits when you got back?"

"They sent me for ten sessions with a psych doctor at the VA, but that only helped so much. Then I started getting immune to the pills they gave me, so I had to find something stronger myself. I'm not proud of that, but I feel like I'm living in a bad dream and I just can't wake up."

"Man, I didn't know how bad the stress was for you. Things are bound to get better. They've just gotta. I'm gonna talk to some of the folks I know down at the NAACP to see if they can help get you back on track. I can't guarantee anything, but I'm willing to try."

"John, I appreciate any kind of help," Jimmy said respectfully. "So how's Cheryl holding up these days?"

"She's still Cheryl as far as I can see—quick-witted, with reflexes like a cheetah."

The waitress returned with two hot plates of food, Jimmy's first real meal in three days.

"That's my Cheryl. The Good Book said we're supposed to be slow to speak and quick to hear. I think Cheryl missed Sunday School that day."

"Ha! I think you're right, 'cause lately she's even had words for the Right Reverend Falls."

"My, my, my. She's getting worse in her old age. I guess I can take the blame for that. I've taken her through a lot over the past year or so. I don't know how she put up with me as long as she did. Outside of my little benefits check, she was covering all the bills. It wasn't that I was trying to be a slacker. I just couldn't pull it together enough to look for steady work again. Once she moved out, I didn't have enough money to keep the apartment up by myself, so I lost it too."

"Jimmy. What happened that night when Cheryl moved back home? I mean, she won't say a peep about it. I figure it must have been a humdinger for her to only take their clothes and a few trinkets and leave everything else behind."

"Honestly, John, I don't remember," Jimmy said as a tear welled up in his eye. "All I can say is that I must have had one of my flashbacks and it just proved to be the straw that broke the camel's back. From what I gather, she probably had every right to call the cops on me that night, but she just didn't do it."

"Do you still love my sister, man?"

"Yeah, with all my heart. I know she loves me, too. I just don't know how to show her love anymore, you know. Besides, I think that this time I pushed her to a place that not even love can bring her back from, or at least not my love. It would take a work from The Man Upstairs to bring her back to me. Heck, I'm trying to get back to me."

"Have you ever shared any of this with Cheryl?"

"She knows some things, but I can't bare my soul to her over all of this, man. She already thinks I'm crazy. I don't want her to see me as weak, too."

"Sho you right, man. Sho you right."

The two men completed the rest of their meal in silence. Both were contemplating the details of the conversation and wondering if maybe too much had been said. Jimmy opened up his heart wide to another brother for the first time since coming home to the States. John had listened more intently than he ever had before. He now felt a sense of torn obligation to another brother's sense of existence, and to his own sister's happiness. John had been watching in silence as Cheryl had started to come undone. Just as

Jimmy's love had been contagious to her, so had his sorrow. Cheryl had been holding on to too much pain, too many secrets. For John, talking to Jimmy had now given him a deeper understanding of his sister's heart.

John knew better now that given Jimmy's mental condition, maybe it was not the time for him and Cheryl to reconcile. However, maybe John could do something else to help reconnect the other missing pieces of his sister's heart – so she could really start to put her life together again.

The waitress returned with the check and a to-go box with another meal for Jimmy. After settling the tab, John handed Jimmy a $5 bill to cover two nights at the shelter. Already out the door, the two exchanged a soul-brothers handshake and turned to part their separate ways.

"Oh, John!" Jimmy shouted back.

"Yeah, man?"

"Tell my little girl happy birthday for me, will ya?"

"Sho you right, man. Sho you right."

With only a half hour left before Bethesda dismissed its parishioners, John decided to just grab a parking spot in the church's lot, giving him a few minutes to map out a strategy of how to free Cheryl into her truth without causing her any more pain. The windows of the church were open so completely that by default John heard the last few minutes of the sermon.

"Brothers and sisters," Reverend Falls continued, "it's one thing to have something and then miss its presence when it's taken away. In that case, we can usually be honest with ourselves about how much we long for it since it's been gone. But it's something else when we try to convince ourselves that we didn't need it in the first place. Because of pride, and sometimes fear, we tell ourselves the lie that our lives were just as fulfilled without it—without the job, without the house, without that spouse.

"For example, some of you want a car but don't have one because you've convinced yourselves that it isn't worth the cost, that you can live without it. But how many witnesses do I have that a car makes your life a whole lot easier? You don't have to worry about bumming a ride with someone or seeing your bus transfer run out before you finish all your errands."

The congregation buzzed with chuckles and amens.

"Some of you see love the same way—as a want, but not a need. You never let true love penetrate your heart because needing real love means you're vulnerable or even weak without it. Need takes us beyond the surface of what we think love looks like, straight to the core of our hearts. Unfortunately, many people go around wearing an imaginary shield like they're immune to real love, like they're the only ones in the world who can live without it—when the reality is that they are the very people who need love the most. They're simply too afraid to admit it.

"These people tend to go through life as if everything is peachy without love because they made up their minds that the real thing was just too hard to come by. Like that car, it just costs too much. Then one day, out of the blue, something or someone comes along and reminds them of how wonderful things could really be. I'm talking about real love, y'all!

"Whatever happened to real love? I'm talking about the kind of love that goes beyond false pretenses and the secrets we keep to save face. I'm talking about the real kind of love that says, 'I love you enough to tell you the truth because keeping a lie is not only hurting me, but secretly harming you.' Yes, we all may best relate to this kind of love in the context of a man and a woman, but what about this kind of love toward ourselves and toward our fellow man? This kind of love sets us free!"

Even in the car, Reverend Falls's words were hitting home for John. He knew Cheryl was keeping a secret about what happened between her and Jimmy the night of the big storm. He also knew that his near-sainthood mother was keeping a secret from Cheryl.

In John's eyes, both women probably thought they were doing the noble thing by preventing others from being hurt. Somehow, though, they missed how much their nobility was suffocating them or subliminally harming the ones they meant to protect. Even John, in his simple-minded view of the world, knew that both women needed help reconnecting to love, real love—if not to embrace it, to at least be freed by it.

Reverend Falls's sermon came to a close, and the rousing benediction hymn could be heard from down the street. The double doors opened and an assembly line of congregants began to file out of the sanctuary like an army of retrained recruits.

John double-parked in front of the church to wait for Ruthie and Yvonne to emerge. He waved to catch their attention.

Yvonne gave a quick goodbye to her friends, while Ruthie paused to greet Reverend Falls and her fellow members of the Willing Workers Committee.

"Hi, Uncle John," Yvonne said, climbing into the backseat.

"Hey, what's happening, Vonnie? How was church?"

"It was fine."

"Any more problems out of your little friend?" John asked teasingly.

"Who, Tommy Stokes? No way! He's not my friend. Besides, he didn't come today. They're away at their family reunion."

"You sure know a lot about his whereabouts to say he's not your friend."

"That's exactly why I know. You have to keep a lookout for your enemies!"

"Girl, you're a mess," John said, laughing at the same time. "Hey, I got a little secret for you."

"Not you, too!"

"Whatcha mean, me too?"

"Never mind, Uncle John."

"Anyway . . . I saw your Daddy today."

"You did? Where?"

"Not too far from here. We had breakfast together."

"You should've come back to get me. Does he live around here? What did he say?"

"Well, he kind of lives around here. He did give me a message for you, though."

"Really? What is it?"

"He said, 'Tell my little girl happy birthday for me.'"
"He did? He remembered! Sometimes I just want to run away to find him. Uncle John, do you think Daddy can come to my birthday dinner next Sunday? Mama says I can make a list of how I want to celebrate. I want to put Daddy on the list. He can be my special guest. I just don't think she'll tell me yes, but if you ask her for me, maybe there's a chance."

"Are you trying to get me involved in your dirty work?"

"Well, kind of."

"I guess that's just proof that we really are related," John said, chuckling. "I'll ask your Mom, but I'm not making any promises. So don't go being all disappointed if it doesn't work out, okay?"

"Okay."

The secret pact was sealed as Ruthie approached the car. John turned down the WVON blues segment playing on the radio as a sign of respect. The two exchanged greetings as Ruthie closed her door. The view of Bethesda faded slowly into the rearview mirror.

John silenced himself completely, contemplating the right time and words to reveal his discovery to Ruthie. She was equally reserved, reflecting on the day's sermon.

"It's funny how you never miss love until you're reminded of how long it's been since you've had love. Funny isn't it?" Ruthie said, almost rhetorically.

"You don't miss a lot of things till they're gone," John said.

"No. That's not what I mean."

"Isn't it the same thing?"

"Not at all, John. On the one hand, you're missing what you forgot you even needed. On the other hand, you're missing something you once had."

"Mama, I'm just saying that sometimes those can be one and the same. Say, for instance, Yvonne lost her favorite doll."

"Uncle John, I'm too big for dolls now," Yvonne chimed in.

"I'm just using you as an example. Just play along for a minute."

John turned back to Ruthie. "So once she's lost it and some time has passed, she starts to forget that she even liked playing with dolls—like she just did. Then, say for instance I was going through some old things in the basement years later and stumbled across her favorite doll again. Once I brought it back to her, wouldn't she remember that she had missed it all that time?"

"I don't know about that one, John," Ruthie said. "It just seems to me that if something was tucked away that long, sooner or later Yvonne would just get over it. I think she would just go on living her life as usual without the doll."

"Life as usual. Is that what you call it?" John asked in a concessional tone. "Okay, Mama. You win this round."

"What do you mean by this round? You make me think you're

116

coming back for round two," Ruthie said sarcastically. "Watch yourself. You know I was trained by Joe Louis himself."

"Well, then I really tip my gloves to you, Mama."

John chose to return to the solitude of his thoughts for the remainder of the ride. There was no sense pushing the envelope if he wasn't ready to make a full delivery. Perhaps this brief conversation with Ruthie would be enough of an introductory buffer for the one he really wanted to have, even needed to have, with his mother. Moments later the car pulled up in front of 1047 Lexington Lane. Ruthie and Yvonne went inside while John scoped out a place to park.

Inside, Cheryl had already given Ruthie a head start by reheating most of their Sunday dinner: spaghetti, fresh string beans, and johnnycakes. Thanks to Cheryl, catfish fillets were seasoned and breaded and a few fresh green tomatoes had been plucked that morning from Ruthie's backyard.

"Hi there, Cheryl," Ruthie said, making her way into the kitchen. "Thanks for getting things started for Mama. Now all I have to do is fry the fish and the tomatoes. Dinner should be ready in about a half hour."

"Not a problem, Mama." Cheryl turned and touched Yvonne's left cheek. "Hi, my Yvonne," she said. "How was church today?"

"It was fine, Mama," Yvonne replied. "No sign of Tommy Stokes!"

"Girl, you and that little Tommy Stokes. One of these days, you just might like him more than you hate him."

"Never!"

"Yeah, we'll see," Cheryl said. "Go on upstairs and get out of those church clothes. Put on some play clothes for dinner. You can stay dressed up next Sunday for your big day."

"Okay, Mama."

"Cheryl, you missed a good sermon this morning," Ruthie said, washing her hands and tucking her head through her flowered print apron.

"Oh, yeah?"

"Yep. Reverend Falls taught about love today."

"Then that's confirmation that I picked the right day to stay at home."

"Oh, Cheryl, don't be such a Scrooge. Besides, he wasn't just talking about the romantic kind of love, but about loving ourselves and one another.

"I was just telling John that it's funny how you never miss love until you're reminded of how long it's been since you've had it. Then, John told me that we don't miss a lot of things until they're gone. Which one of us do you think is right?"

"Sounds like you're both saying the same thing to me," Cheryl replied dubiously.

"Oh, there you go, too. I guess I'm the only one who separates the two in my mind. It's just easier that way. It's like keeping two piles of laundry, your whites on one side and your colors on the other. Both are still clothes that you wore and need to wash. But one pile is basic and plain; ain't no frills in white clothing. White clothes are easier to get dirty, but they're also easier to clean. You just throw some bleach on them and they're good as new.

"Colors, on the other hand, add all this life to your wardrobe. Colored clothes show your personality, how you're feeling on a particular day. But it's harder to maintain their brightness. Sooner or later the colors will fade away and things won't look the same anyway. So, if you're someone like me who prefers to keep things basic and consistent, then you don't get your hopes all up for colors to always look the same 'cause you never really allow yourself to feel like you needed colors in the first place."

"Wow. It sounds like you got a whole lot out of today's message, Mama. I think I heard it better from you than I would have from Reverend Falls," Cheryl said. "Now I see why they used to call you Truthie Ruthie. You just tell it like it is, don't ya, Mama?"

"Hey, what can I say?"

"But you're wearing blue today, Mama. That's a color. Plus your apron has all kinds of colorful flowers on it," Cheryl said. "Looks like sometimes colors are worth the troubled maintenance."

"Sometimes," Ruthie recanted.

Sheila slipped in quietly in the midst of their discourse.

"Hey, everybody."

"Hey there, yourself," Ruthie replied.

"Cheryl, you got a minute?" Sheila asked. "I need to show you something."

"Oh, okay."

"It's upstairs."

"I guess that's code for I want to show my sister something without my Mama peeping in on it," Ruthie said.

Sheila turned from the kitchen doorway and headed upstairs without even a hint of a rebuttal. Puzzled by her sister's behavior, Cheryl quietly followed Sheila up to her room. Sheila closed the door behind Cheryl. The sisters sat side by side on Sheila's bed.

"I was going to wait until after dinner to say something, but I can't hold it anymore."

"Can't hold what anymore?" Cheryl asked. "I thought you wanted to show me something."

"Not exactly. I have a problem. Well, maybe—I don't know, but I'm pretty sure I do."

"What's up with all the riddles in this house today? What are you talking about, Shay?"

"I don't know how to say this."

"Say what?"

"Well . . . I'm—I'm—I'm late."

"Late for what?" Cheryl asked, holding her head sideways. "Wait a minute. You're not the type of late I think you are, are you? Are you talking about your Aunt Flo?"

"I'm scared, Cheryl. Don't judge me. I don't know what to do. With all the arguments me and Mama have had about Bobby, I can't even begin to know how to tell her something like this."

"When did all of this happen? How? I mean, I know how, but you kept telling Mama that there was no way anything inappropriate was going on, and now this!"

"Don't be angry with me, Cheryl."

"I'm not angry with you about possibly becoming a mother. I'm angry that you were so blinded by the way *you* wanted to see things that you caused all this confusion with Mama. Heck, you haven't even apologized since the last blowup, and now you want to throw on the fire that you've been lying to her the entire time? That she was actually right?"

"I know. I know," Sheila said, beginning to cry. "I just hate that she's right all the time. I love him, and I know that once he finds out, he'll want to marry me."

"Whoa! Wait a minute. You don't know what you think you know, Shay. Before you go barking up that tree, you need to be more sure about what and who you're dealing with in this situation. I don't think you know Bobby nearly as much as you think you do."

"I know him plenty. We've been dating for six months now and he told me he loves me. I didn't do anything with him until earlier this summer. He respects me, Cheryl. He's been nothing but a gentleman the entire time."

"Shay, how much of a gentleman could he be when he's never come in the house to properly meet your family? And why is it that he can never drive you all the way to your destination in his car? And why is it that he only has time for you at the crack of dawn or really late at night?"

"He's busy. He works full time and he's in school just like me. That's where we met. You make it sound like I should be suspicious of something. Everything's on the up-and-up with Bobby, Cheryl. I just know it."

"Shay, you may not know half of what you think you do. You just don't know how much he may be keeping from you, that's all I'm saying. How late are you, anyway?"

"About a month."

"Oh, my God! Have you ever been late like this before?"

"I used to be irregular in high school, but the doctor said that I was fine now."

"Well, you need to see the doctor again before you say anything to Bobby. Shay, I didn't want to say anything to you about this. As a matter of fact, I promised that I wouldn't, but I don't see how I can keep it from you at this point. Yvonne told me that—"

"Mama! Mama! Mama!"

Cheryl jumped up off the bed, flung open the door, and rushed down the hall toward Yvonne's screams. Sheila wiped her tears and followed Cheryl. They ended up in the doorway of the bathroom, where Yvonne was sitting on the toilet with tears of her own.

"Mama, it's here! What do I do?"

"Girl, you scared me half to death. I thought something terrible had happened.

"My baby's a young woman now! Remember, this is what we've been talking about for the past year or so. Don't worry about a thing. Take a shower. I'll bring you a change of clothes and the pack of maxi pads we've been saving for your special day."

"Mama, I'm scared."

"You have nothing to fear. Besides, one day the sight of this may be a welcome relief. Won't it, Shay? Looks like your niece found what you may have lost," Cheryl said under her breath.

"That's not funny, Cheryl."

"I never said it was funny. Come on, let's step out of the bathroom and give this young woman her privacy. Vonnie, I'll be right back with your things," Cheryl said, closing the door behind her.

"Shay, we'll have to finish our talk later."

"There's no need. I know where you stand."

"No. No, you don't. I'm on your side. You just seem to think that people who are against you are for you, and those for you are against you. I just hope and pray you learn the difference. When are you going to the doctor?"

"I have an appointment tomorrow morning."

"Good. I'll go with you, if you want me to?"

"You'd do that for me?"

"That's what big sisters do."

* * *

Sunday dinner was a welcome norm amidst the family's unsettling ebbs and flows. Given the sudden change of life events, and the absence of any special guests, Cheryl invited Yvonne to a seat at the dining room table. Yvonne sat stoically and withdrawn, hoping to minimize the stares of those who were certain to instinctively notice the change in her body. Sheila did the same.

Papa Boyd had already dug into the fried green tomatoes as John slipped in just in time for the end of Ruthie's grace. Cheryl sat at the ready as mediator this time around, leaving the formal niceties to Ruthie and Mr. Pratt.

"I tell you, Ms. Ruthie, this is a mighty fine spread you have for us today—a mighty fine spread."

"Oh, thank you, Mr. Pratt."

"I guarantee it must have taken you hours to pull this one off. Thanks for going through all the trouble," he said. "Will someone please pass the fish?"

"It's no trouble at all. I love cooking for the household. That includes you too, Mr. Pratt. I just wish you'd bless us with your presence more often during the week."

"Oh, I've got plenty to eat in my room. I just like to indulge in a good home-cooked meal now and again. Plus, I enjoy being in the midst of you fine people here today."

"How kind of you to say."

"I wouldn't say it if it wasn't true, Ms. Ruthie. Spaghetti, someone?" He looked up suddenly. "Oh, did anyone hear screaming right before dinnertime? I thought I heard a scream," he said.

"Everything's just fine, Mr. Pratt," Cheryl jumped in. "Just us ladies doing what ladies do. We're sorry if we disturbed you. There's no need to worry about us."

"No worry at all."

"We all appreciate that, Mr. Pratt," Ruthie said. "So, *ladies*, is everything okay now? You all seem so quiet today."

"Yes, Mama," Cheryl said. "Everything's just fine."

As conversation resettled, John precariously chose the moment to set the stage for round two with Ruthie. He was hoping that an open forum would diffuse any impact from his final blow.

"So, Mama, did you give any more thought to my insight on Reverend Falls's sermon?" John asked.

"Your insight? You weren't even there to hear his sermon."

"I was parked by the church's windows, Mama. I could hear him loud and clear."

"Oh, then I stand corrected. Someone pass me another johnnycake," Ruthie said, breaking her awkwardness and avoiding another embarrassing Sabbath. "So what did you hear?"

"He said that folks often think of love as a want and not a need. So when a person thinks that way, it's easy for them to ignore the importance of true love. It's like the person chooses to do without the passion that true love brings."

"Sounds a bit complicated to me, John," Cheryl said. "How deep are you going here? We've still got young ears at the table."

"I understand him," Mr. Pratt said, barely above a whisper. "I think I've done that myself. After I lost my family, part of me shut down to love. I guess I did it on purpose. It was easier to think I didn't need it anymore. It just hurt too bad to want it."

"Wow, Mr. Pratt," Cheryl said. "So have you been successful? I mean, with convincing your heart that you don't need love?"

"Not one bit. That's why I'm sitting here with you fine people on today, because I keep trying to push past the pain. Some days I'm not so good at it—most days. But the truth is everyone needs love. It's a wounded soul who thinks he doesn't need love, and a scared soul who doesn't even want it."

"Man, Mr. Pratt, you could give Reverend Falls a run for his money with that one. That's out of sight," John said. "That's heavy stuff, man. You don't say much, but when you do, it's right up there with Dr. King. I respect that, man."

"I respect you, too, Mr. John," Mr. Pratt replied. "Well, dinner was delicious and the conversation delightful, but I must retire for the evening. Ms. Ruthie, thank you and the family for a wonderful afternoon."

"Oh, all right, Mr. Pratt," Ruthie said. "Good afternoon to you as well."

Even with his proclamation of needing love, Mr. Pratt's tender heart could only take so much of it at any given time. He quickly excused himself, leaving the Boyds to finish their meal alone.

Dinner completed, Ruthie, Sheila, and Yvonne went into the kitchen to put away the leftovers and wash the dishes. John quietly reached for Cheryl's arm right as she rose from her seat at the table.

"Hey, Sis, can I talk to you for a second?"

"Sure. What's up?"

"I ran into Jimmy again today."

"Yeah?"

"Yeah. We had breakfast together and had a chance to talk."

"Oh, really now?"

"Hear me out. I don't know what all went down between the two of you, and from his own lips he said he doesn't remember but is pretty sure you could have called the cops. So believe me, I get it that things aren't peachy keen for you guys. But just because your marriage is shaky doesn't mean he stops being Yvonne's daddy."

"I know," Cheryl said nonchalantly.

"I'm only bringing it up because Yvonne's birthday is next Sunday."

"I know that, too. Trust me. I was there the day she was born."

"Relax, Sis. Just relax."

"I am relaxed, John. Will you just get to the point already?"

"Okay. Bottom line is he misses Yvonne, and Yvonne wants him to come to her birthday dinner."

"She does not."

"Yes, she does. She asked me to ask you because she didn't think you would tell her yes. Now I see why."

"What is that supposed to mean?"

"I'm just saying, Cheryl. You just seem a bit hardhearted to the whole thing right from jump street. You barely want to hear me out now, so I can only imagine how you would have replied to her."

"I don't know about all of this, John. I'm not ready."

"That's you. What about Yvonne? She told me she's thought about running away to find him."

"Oh, my God," Cheryl said, hiding her face in her hands.

"Look, Sis, I'll be right here the whole time. You won't have to worry about a thing. I'll bring him here in time for dinner, or even just cake and ice cream if that's what you prefer. Then I'll take him right out of here.

"Cheryl, let Jimmy come. You wouldn't want someone withholding your father from you, would you?"

"Let me think on it."

"Okay, but don't wait too long. It may take me a couple days to track him down again. He doesn't have a steady spot to stay at yet," John said, starting to stand from his seat. He changed his mind.

"Cheryl, I really wish you would tell me what happened between you two. Maybe I wouldn't push you so hard if I knew. All I have to go on is what I see in front of me—a wounded soldier and a little girl who misses her daddy."

Cheryl's thoughts were moving a mile a minute, so fast she couldn't seem to grasp one of them. Here she was with yet another tug-of-war, this time between her personal wants and her daughter's needs. Cheryl had already decided she no longer wanted Jimmy's love, and she surely didn't feel she needed it—but then there was Yvonne. She was becoming a young woman now and needed her father's love now more than ever. How could the two planes coexist? How could she and her daughter have experienced the same thing and have two totally different points of view?

Having dropped his first bomb of the evening, John moved to the next item on his agenda: Ruthie Boyd's mystery box.

Leaning into the kitchen doorway, John asked, "Mama, do you think I can grab a few minutes of your time when you're finished in here?"

"Why? What's up, John?"

"I just need to talk to you about something."

"Talk away."

"I'd rather it be just me and you. I'll be on the porch, Mama."

"Okay. I'll be there in a minute."

Ruthie dried her hands on her apron, draped it on a hook near the pantry, and gave Sheila and Yvonne her last clean-up instructions before leaving the kitchen.

"You all right, Cheryl?" Ruthie asked in passing. "You seem a little shell-shocked sitting there at the table."

"Oh. Yes, Mama. I'm fine. Just thinking about something is all."

"All right, then. I'm going out on the porch to see what your brother's so anxious to tell me. Let my grandbaby bring us out some lemonade when she finishes in the kitchen, you hear?"

"Yes, Mama."

Ruthie exited the front screen door to find John leaning over the banister of the porch.

"So what's up, Doc? It seems like you've got urgent business to tend to for a change."

John slowly turned to Ruthie and pulled out a small envelope that he had tucked away in his shirt's breast pocket. He handed it to her, postage side up. Upon contact, the envelope immediately felt familiar. She glanced down at the handwriting and then the postmark: 1943. Her heart started racing. Her mouth went dry. How could he have found this letter? It was buried so, so far away. No one went into that part of the basement anymore, not even John. It was dark, damp, filled with spiders and cobwebs. This letter represented a separate pile of emotional laundry all its own, and no one ever wanted to touch it, let alone wash it. There were just too many colors there, and everyone knows that bright colors bleed. If he found this letter, then surely he had found the others, and the pictures, and the engagement ring. Her heart was skipping now. Her mind was running. Maybe it was a fluke. Maybe this was just one of the innocent love letters that most girls got back then. Maybe this one letter got mysteriously dislodged from the rest, like a single sock separated from the rest of the load. Maybe.

With moist palms, Ruthie found the strength to open the single letter. The first few lines read, "Ruthie, I miss you and our baby girl so much. I'm counting the days until I come home and we can be a real family."

Ruthie lost the strength to stand and slumped down into the cedar chair. There was no momentum left in her to rock back and forth. No need to anyway, seeing that the back and front of her life had suddenly come crashing in together. The past and future were now colliding in the middle.

John's voice faded out more and more from Ruthie's mind. She heard bits and pieces of him explaining how his curiosity for old blues records led him to the dark places of her memories. He told her how he'd found her most prized possession—her mother's old trunk, and in it, the crate that held her high school diploma showing that she'd graduated first in her class, her treasured photos, and her love letters from Monroe. He told her that the first letter he read asked about "the baby" and that its date led him on a quest for answers he knew she would never share. John explained that, at first, he'd hoped he would just find out some lively tidbits about her, then thought maybe something historic would surface. So rather than asking permission, he organized the letters by their dates and continued to read them. He read until he saw it in plain English, and in Monroe Jackson's own handwriting, that Cheryl was really his daughter. John told her that he had been so torn over the past few days between confronting her like a man and just minding his own business like her son. He told it all.

Ruthie remained perfectly still, her eyes glued to the words written on the page as if re-reading them would take her back in time and away from this present-day truth. She longed for the days with Monroe, when her life was simple and carefree. She mourned for the scared nineteen-year-old girl whose life was turned upside down in one moment on lovers' lane. She remembered the sacrificial decision of a young woman in hopes of creating a better life for her child. All of her daydreams had turned into nightmares.

John's voice became clear to Ruthie just long enough to hear him say, "Mama, I don't know why you chose to never say anything, but I think Cheryl needs to know. And I think you need to be freed from this secret. Now, either you say something to her, or I will."

As if doused with a glass of cold water, Ruthie returned to Lexington Lane with the creak of the screen door and the sound of Yvonne's hopeful voice.

"Here's your lemonade, Granny."

"Not tonight, baby. Not tonight."

STORM CLOUDS RISE

The next morning, Sheila and Cheryl slipped out the back entrance of the house before anyone noticed. They caught the first bus they could to the doctor's office on State Street. Cheryl wore blue denim bell-bottoms, platform shoes, and a floral print top. Sheila had on a tie-dyed dress and sandals. Both were now sporting Afros and dark shades, perhaps as a disguise to blend in among the other people downtown.

"Do you have an appointment, ma'am?" the desk clerk asked Cheryl as she entered the clinic.

"Oh, I'm not here for myself. I'm here with my sister."

Cheryl turned to look for Sheila, who was straggling in behind her, too nervous to even approach the desk.

"I have an appointment with Dr. Davis. A checkup is all," Sheila insisted.

"Alrighty then. Please sign in for me here, and the doctor will see you shortly."

Cheryl placed her hand on Sheila's shoulder for support, then guided her to a seat in the waiting area.

"Sheila, whatever happens today, just know that I'm here for you."

"Thanks, Sis."

The two spent the next fifteen minutes sitting in silence. Cheryl flipped aimlessly through the latest issue of *National Geographic*, just because it was there. Sheila glanced at the various prenatal posters on the walls, trying desperately to keep her heart from jumping out of her chest. She had dreamed of being a mother— someday, but today was about seven years ahead of her perfect schedule. She always planned to finish college, get a good job in marketing, and *then* start her happily-ever-after with a husband and two kids. This would throw off the entire plan. How would Robert react? Would he want to get married? Should she keep it? How would her mother react?

Sheila never questioned whether Ruthie loved her. She had no doubt that Ruthie would guide her through raising a child, but, boy, it would be years before she would let her live this one down. Years.

"Ms. Boyd, the doctor will see you now," a nurse said to Sheila.

"Do you want me to come back there with you?" Cheryl asked Sheila.

"Actually, ma'am, Dr. Davis's policy is that only a husband or mother can go into the exam room with her."

"It's okay, Cheryl," Sheila whispered.

"I'll be right here when you come out, Shay," Cheryl reassured her.

Cheryl sat twiddling with her nails and praying for a false-positive result. How would Sheila take the news if she was expecting? How would their mother respond? And how—how in the world— could she break the news to Sheila about Bobby's extracurricular activities? There was no way that Yvonne would make up a story like that, so it had to be true. But how could she tell Sheila without breaking her oath to Yvonne?

"Excuse me, Miss, is someone sitting here?"

"No," Cheryl replied to the woman now standing before her. "My sister was, but she's with the doctor now."

"Oh, thank you. The waiting room is pretty crowded for so early in the day."

"Mm-hmm," Cheryl replied, trying to be polite without striking up a conversation.

"My husband went to park the car," the lady continued. "He should be inside any minute. I don't know where he's going to sit, though. So you like *National Geographic*, my sister?"

"No, not really. The pictures just caught my eye, but I'd love to travel to some of these remote places someday."

"Oh, I love to travel. My husband and I just got back from a few days out East with my parents. I started to feel a bit nauseous while I was there and my mother just insisted that I get to the doctor immediately. She's so ready to be a grandmother."

"How nice."

"I hope you brought an umbrella with you today," the woman said. "Looks like rain."

Just then, the clinic door opened as if on cue for an answered prayer. A man entered, and the woman seated beside Cheryl waved her hand to catch his attention in the crowded waiting room. He began walking across the room. Cheryl glanced up from the magazine just in time to identify the body. It was Bobby, and he was just as good as dead to Cheryl.

"Here's my husband now," the woman proudly announced. "Honey, I'm sorry, but there are no more seats."

Bobby made eye contact with Cheryl and froze within himself. The two had only a few brief encounters while Sheila was getting in or out of his car, but enough for Cheryl to recognize him immediately. Cheryl decided to play it cool, like a game of chess, waiting to craft her next move based on his initial reaction.

Sheepishly Bobby ignored Cheryl's presence and told his wife he would sit in the car until it was her turn, due to the overcrowding of course. He then made an immediate about-face out the door.

A while later, Sheila emerged from the exam area with a half-smile on her face as she walked toward Cheryl.

"Well, the doctor gave me a urine test," Sheila said quietly.

"And?"

"It was negative."

"Thank God!" Cheryl sighed.

"He took a blood sample, too, just to be 100 percent sure. But I can come back Friday on my lunch break for those results. So I guess there's nothing to tell Robert after all."

"Good! Let's go."

"You ladies have a good day," said the woman as Cheryl stood from her seat. "If you don't mind, if you see my husband anywhere outside can you tell him a seat opened up beside me. As a matter of fact, his name is Robert, too. Sometimes I call him Bobby for short."

Cheryl glanced at the woman as if her words were mindless and deranged. She grabbed Sheila's arm quickly and nudged her toward the exit.

Now outside the clinic, Cheryl and Sheila repositioned their shades to block out the sun. Just as Sheila was putting on her sunglasses, a silhouette several doors down the street caught her eye.

"Oh my God, girl, I think that's Robert," Sheila announced to Cheryl.

"Oh, Lord help me today."

"Girl, what should I do? I don't know if he saw me."

"Let's just assume that this guy is not *your* Robert, and start walking to the bus stop."

"I want to see him, but I don't want him to know I just came out of the women's clinic, Cheryl."

"Sheila, let's go."

"Wait a minute," Sheila said, starting to slowly walk toward the man leaning on a black Nova in the middle of the block.

"Come on, Sheila. Let's go."

"Cheryl, wait a minute."

"Sheila. Sheila!"

Sheila continued her walk toward him, with each step feeling more and more confident that the man was Robert, her Robert. She felt relieved that the scare was behind her and envisioned that the best was just a few steps before her.

"Robert!" Sheila shouted with her arms already extended to embrace him.

"Sheila! What are you doing here?" Robert asked, pulling away.

"Never mind all of that. I'm downtown with Cheryl, that's all. We were about to walk to the bus stop when I noticed you leaning on your car. Maybe you can give us a lift back to the house.

"So what brings you downtown anyway? Looks like you're waiting for something or maybe somebody."

Cheryl walked up in time to hear Sheila's last few statements. Her eyes met Robert's again and she instantly reengaged in her last chess move.

"Yeah, Robert, what brings you downtown?" Cheryl interrogated.

"Well, I, uh—uh—I—um—" Robert muttered, searching for syllables.

"Robert, I don't know why you chose to keep this secret," Cheryl said, "but I think she should know. Either you tell her, or I will."

"Tell me what? What are you talking about, Cheryl? What's going on here, Bobby?"

"Sheila, I'm, uh—I'm, uh, mar . . ." Robert's voice lost its smooth, mellow strength.

"I don't think Sheila could hear what you said, Robert," Cheryl continued to badger.

"Sheila, I'm—I'm married. I—I should have said something sooner, but things between us were going so smooth. I wouldn't have usually done something like this, but my wife and I were going through a rough patch. Sorry."

"Robert! Robert!" The woman from the clinic shouted down the street. "It's time for my appointment."

Sheila turned in time to see that the woman speaking was the same woman from the waiting room. Her mouth dropped open, her eyes welled up with tears, and a pain hit her chest like a million bee stings. The blood flowing to Sheila's heart seemed confused and without direction. Her breath became shallow and grim. Her life had suddenly shifted into slow motion.

Sheila knew what she heard Robert say, and knew that she had just seen his wife—*his wife*. Now she saw him walking toward *her*.

How could any of this be possible? Just six months before, Sheila was still one of "the good girls" in church. She had barely dated and had never even been kissed. She was always determined to wait for the right guy: someone smart, focused, clean-cut, and kind. She never thought she had to add single to the list. She felt foolish for the first time, and filled with a palpable shame that not even her sunglasses could hide.

"Sheila, I'm so sorry," Cheryl said taking her little sister into her arms. "I'm so sorry."

Sheila sobbed into Cheryl's embrace, standing in the middle of State Street for the entire world to see. She felt full and empty all at once—full of hurt, pain, and confusion, and empty because her purity had been swindled away from her. How could she be so smart and so dumb at the same time?

Hoping to avoid an uglier scene between Robert and his wife, Cheryl walked Sheila in the opposite direction, cradling Sheila's head on her right shoulder.

"Please don't tell Mama, Cheryl. Please."

"I won't. I promise."

* * *

At the house, Ruthie was already in the basement sorting laundry—whites over here, colors over there. She slept lighter than a pea on a pillow the entire night, and awoke just as restless. Ruthie had stripped the linens from every bed, every towel from both bathrooms, and removed the drapery from all the windows, even Mr. Pratt's room. Everything that had been neatly arranged and safely collecting dust in its place was being moved and cleaned. If she had to come clean, the whole house was coming clean with her.

Ruthie called Reverend Falls and asked him to be present for support when she told Cheryl the news. He would only be available the following Sunday, which meant that all of this had to come to a head on poor Yvonne's birthday. Should she should wait until another time? No. Ruthie had already waited thirty years, long enough, and the stress of all this exposure was making her burst at the seams. No more secrets. No more splitting hairs between hurt and harm.

Ruthie closed the washing machine lid on her third load of laundry. From the corner of her eye, she saw her mother's old brown leather trunk, on the floor beside John's wooden secondhand desk. Why did he have such a sense of curiosity about everything? Why did he have to go digging through the back storage room of the basement into *her* things? Why did he have to go rummaging through the back room of her mind? Better yet, why hadn't she locked the trunk? Couldn't John just tuck this away in a storage compartment in his own mind? It would be easier, but then that wouldn't be fair. Everyone wasn't built the way she was. Ruthie knew she had a special gift for locking things away in mental compartments, but somehow this time she forgot about the lock.

Ruthie took a seat at John's desk and opened the trunk. The crate with all of her memories was sitting there clear as day. She reached for the manila envelope and pulled out the time-worn photos of her and Monroe. Prom night 1941. Earnestine's graduation party. Her with Monroe in his naval uniform. She saw her old red velvet ring box—the white gold solitaire, one-third carat diamond ring still inside. Ruthie was holding it in her hand again for the first time in twenty years, which was when she got it back from her mother and swore to tuck it away for a lifetime.

The damage was done now. The secret was out. Yet maybe she could convince John to keep it under wraps a little while longer. How long was a little while, though? What once constituted "a little while" had changed so much through the years. Ruthie originally planned to only keep things from Cheryl while she was a baby. Then she decided to wait until Cheryl grew past her childhood— those were such formative years. Then a little while became at least until she finished high school. How devastating it would have been for Cheryl to be in search of her identity as a young woman only to learn that everything she already knew about herself was based on a lie! Then a little while just didn't seem to matter anymore. Cheryl was grown now, with a family and history of her own. It seemed to Ruthie that the right time to tell Cheryl was gone, long gone, until now.

Chapter Fourteen

WORDS WILL EVER HURT ME

Dear Diary,

It's been a little while since I wrote to you. I'm doing a countdown until my 13th birthday. Only three days left! I'm having a party on Sunday. Thelma's coming from next door. JoAnne is coming from church, and my cousin Anne is coming to stay over for the weekend. Uncle John even asked Mama if Daddy can come. I hope so. I sure do hope so.

On another note, everyone in the house is acting weird. Auntie Sheila's been crammed up in her room since Monday. She even skipped a couple days of work. I had to sneak in her closet to get you while she was in the bathroom. I guess now I'll have to hide you somewhere in me and Mama's room. Mama's been strange, too. It's like she wants to say something but doesn't know where to start. And Granny, I think she's acting the strangest of them all. We haven't sat out on the porch one night this entire week. She's been going to the park every day instead. She seems sad. I asked her if she wanted to talk about it with me, but she said it was no big deal. I think it's a big deal all right—a big people's deal. I hope they all get it together before my birthday.

Love,
Yvonne

"Morning," Cheryl said to Yvonne, who was sitting on the porch and slowly closing her diary. "I see you've got an early start today."

"Hi, Mama. Yeah, I guess I'm getting excited about my birthday."

"By right you should be." She took a seat on the step beside Yvonne. "So, I've been reading over your list of birthday demands," she said.

"They're not demands, Mama, just wishes."

"Well, whatever you call them, here's what I can do. We'll put up pink and yellow balloons and streamers in the dining room for decoration. I'll bake your chocolate chip cookies and your Granny will make you a caramel cake. As for a slumber party and pizza, your cousin Anne spending the weekend is about as close to that as you're gonna get. I'll order a pizza for you two Saturday night. By then your hair will have dried so I can hot comb it that afternoon," Cheryl said as she touched Yvonne's two shoulder-length braids.

"Mama, I was happy until you said the last part. I hate getting my hair washed. It always takes *too* long to dry and it always gets *too* tangled."

"And that's why I start on it *two* days before."

"Mama, can I add one more thing to my wish list?"

"What's that?"

"A perm! Please, Mama. Anne has one. She has a kiddie perm in her hair and it's always so pretty."

"Your hair is always so pretty, too, naturally. I don't want all those chemicals in your hair, confusing your cells."

"You make it sound like it's going inside my brain."

"It may as well be. Besides, you're still a little too young for that."

"Mama, I'm *still* too young for stuff?"

"Yes, you are. I know you're getting older, but there's no need to rush things along. Trust me on this one. We'll talk about you getting a perm when it's time for you to start high school next year. I won't promise you anything, but we'll talk about it."

"I guess that's a step at least," Yvonne conceded.

"Hey, Missy, I have another question for you. Your Uncle John told me that you want to invite your father to your birthday party. Is that really true?"

"I want that more than anything else on the list, Mama."

"I don't want to put words in your mouth, but aren't you the least bit concerned about him repeating any of the bad things he did the last time we saw him?"

"Mama, he didn't do anything wrong the last time *I* saw him. All he did was give me a hug and say that he loves me."

"When was this?"

"A few weeks ago, but we didn't want you to get mad so I didn't say anything. I'm sorry."

"Where were you when you saw him? You know what? On second thought, I don't want to know. As long as you felt safe, that's all that matters now."

"Mama, if you were really talking about what he did the night we moved back in with Granny, well, you told me to put it out of my mind. So that's what I did. I stopped thinking about it, so I don't really remember it. I think I just substituted something good in its place."

"I wish it were that easy for me, baby," Cheryl said, fiddling with her fingernails. "So you really want to invite him to your party?"

"Yes, Mama."

"Okay. Then I'll talk to your Uncle John."

"Thank you, Mama," Yvonne said, leaning into her mother's arms. "Thank you! Thank you!"

The remainder of the day was unusually quiet for the Boyds. There was an offbeat atmosphere in the home. Ruthie scurried about from room to room in her yellow housework dress. Up and down the step stool she went, washing windows, rehanging drapery, restocking the linen closet. Sheila came downstairs for tea at noon, still wearing her pajamas. Ruthie had a house rule that no one could walk around all day in bedclothes. She always said that a brand-new day deserved the courtesy of being greeted in clean clothes. Yet Sheila walked about the kitchen, and with not as much as a peep from Ruthie about it.

Papa Boyd sat through a marathon of *The Big Valley*, while John was out doing a double shift of day work at the Trailways bus depot. Cheryl and Yvonne took advantage of the inconsequential day to go shopping for the birthday celebration before returning home to start the evening chore of washing Yvonne's hair.

The next morning John picked up Anne at the depot before heading home from work. She had a short trip from Gray, Indiana, to Chicago.

The anticipation of a new face brought new energy to the home. Ruthie had cooked a special breakfast to welcome her great-niece, and to kick off Yvonne's birthday weekend. Scrambled eggs, grits, country bacon, homemade strawberry preserves, and biscuits were being placed on the dining room table. Yvonne was up early, too, helping Ruthie with the biscuits and setting some aside just for Anne.

John's keys clinked at the front door.

"Look what the wind blew in," Ruthie said, looking at thirteen-year-old Anne for the first time all year. "Look how you've grown. Child, come give your Auntie Ruthie a hug! Ooh, I can hardly believe it," she said, embracing Anne.

"Anne!" Yvonne shouted with excitement.

"Yvonne!"

"Um, Anne, what happened to your face?"

"Oh, that. I just got over the chicken pox. I got them from my little brother, but they're all gone now, Yvonne."

"But you still have some scabs. Can I catch 'em?"

"No, silly. The scabs mean that they've dried up already."

"Yvonne, you've had them already," Ruthie said. "So give her a hug and hush your mouth."

The Boyd house came alive for the first time in days. It got loud all of a sudden. The good kind of loud, like during holidays when all their distant relatives gathered together and loved each other— even if only for a little while.

"Anne, baby, sit down and let me fix you a plate," Ruthie said. "What would you like to eat? We've got eggs, grits, and bacon. Seems like I'm already running low on biscuits."

"No, you're not, Granny. I saved some for Anne on the counter. I'll go get them."

"Oh, that was mighty nice of you, Yvonne. Come on, Anne, and eat."

Breakfast chatter included John telling Papa Boyd about his pickup shift as Cheryl, Sheila, and Ruthie bombarded Anne with questions about her trip to Chicago and her mother Sarah.

"Anne, how's your mother?" Sheila asked Anne.

"Yeah, how is the lone ranger?" Cheryl said sarcastically.

"Cheryl. Don't go starting in on that child," Ruthie said. "She don't have anything to do with you and Sarah not keeping in touch like you should."

After an awkward moment, Anne decided to do the respectful thing and still responded to the big people's questions.

"She's fine," Anne said. "Happy, really."

"Why's that?" Sheila asked.

"'Cause Daddy just bought her a new car. They drove me to the bus station in it."

"A new car, huh?" Cheryl said. "That's nice. What kind of car?"

"I forget the name. It's something that begins with the letter S."

"Is it a Subaru or a Sable?" Sheila said, trying to guess.

"No something like Seville. That's it! It's a Seville," Anne recalled.

"What you say? Go on with your bad self, Sarah," Cheryl said.

"A Seville, huh? What year?" Sheila asked.

"A '73, I guess. Daddy always says he doesn't like leftovers. Not leftover food or hand-me-down clothes. So I'd think he'd be the same way about cars."

"Oh, really?" Cheryl said with slight tension in her tone.

"Enough, Cheryl," Ruthie said. "That's enough."

While Anne ate, John took her bags upstairs to Sheila's room.

"Hurry up, Anne, so we can do something," Yvonne said. "We can go outside or we can play some games. We've got Monopoly, Chinese Checkers, and a couple of puzzles, too."

"I'm coming. Just let me wash my hands." Anne had just stuffed her mouth with the last piece of a biscuit and had Ruthie's homemade preserves stuck to her fingertips.

"I'm full," she said, standing up from her seat at the table. "What can we do if we go outside?"

"I don't know if you still like to do the things I do," Yvonne said. "I like to play Red Light Green Light, four square, Chinese jump rope, hopscotch, and Piggy."

"Can we just jump double Dutch or go to the park?"

"Um, we can go to the park. We need to ask first."

"I know what you two can do," Ruthie interjected, reaching into her wallet for a five-dollar bill. "You can walk up to Fairplay and buy me a gallon of milk, some Vidalia onions, and a bag of white potatoes. I won't mind if you take a scenic route past the candy store or park first, just so long as you're back before lunchtime."

"Thanks, Granny."

"Double check that it's okay with your mama, and you two make sure you stay together."

"We'll do, Granny."

"Thanks, Auntie Ruthie."

Yvonne and Anne started their leisurely walk down Lexington Lane. The two were catching up on what had happened with the rest of their summers. The last time they saw each other was when Anne had spent the night at Yvonne's old apartment—the same night as the big storm.

"So, Yvonne, who else is coming to your party?" Anne asked.

"My friend Thelma is coming from next door, and my friend JoAnne from church will be here, too."

"Anne and JoAnne, that's funny," Anne said. "So it's just gonna be the four of us?"

"No, the whole family will be there."

"By whole family do you mean Cousin Jimmy, too?"

"Yep, that's the plan. Why do you ask?"

"I just thought that after everything that went down that night . . . I—I just didn't expect to see him. That's all."

"Everybody keeps talking about that night like it was so bad."

144

"Everybody like who? It was just you, me, and Cousin Cheryl there, other than Jimmy, and Cheryl made us promise not to tell anyone. I didn't! Besides, I just could hear her crying for help. You're the one who actually saw what happened that night. All I know is that we rushed out of your apartment so fast that I was on a bus back to Gary the next day. So, what did happen that night, Yvonne? You never told me."

"I don't think I remember much."

"How could you not remember? We both heard your father tell Cheryl, 'I'll kill you.' Who can forget hearing that? You were the one who was brave enough to open your parents' bedroom door when we heard your mama crying. You were the one who ran across the hall to get help from your old neighbor. Or did you forget that, too?"

"I *said*, I don't remember much, and that's the truth!"

"All right, Yvonne. Don't cop a 'tude with me. I was just trying to help."

"Sorry. I just don't want to talk about it. Let's just go on to the store."

"Okay, but just because you don't want to remember doesn't mean it didn't happen. You can try to ignore the words people say, but it doesn't mean you didn't hear them. If you wanna walk around like nothin' ever happened, then that's fine with me."

Back at the house, Cheryl prepared herself to talk to Ruthie about inviting Jimmy. She knew Ruthie had never been a big fan of Jimmy's from day one. Ruthie always had a way of implying that he didn't quite measure up to what she saw as being the best for her eldest child. She was never directly rude, per se, just not approving. So when Jimmy had come home from the war a couple years before and started his downward spiral, it had only solidified Ruthie's position. Cheryl remembered clearly the day she told Ruthie they were planning to get married. Ruthie's response was simple and to the point.

"Cheryl, I love you, but I don't like him," Ruthie said. "I can't put my finger on it, but something's just not right, and it may never be right."

Cheryl remembered Ruthie asking her, "Are you pregnant, child?" She even recalled her own coy reply.

"No, Mama. I don't have to be pregnant to decide I want to get married. Every wedding's not a shotgun. We've got hopes and dreams. Unlike you, Mama, I believe in him. I believe in us."

Thinking back to that moment, Cheryl remembered feeling so hurt and rejected by Ruthie. In her heart, she and Jimmy had already become one. So when Ruthie rejected him, in Cheryl's eyes she had automatically rejected her, too.

Maybe things weren't that clear-cut then. Or maybe Ruthie had a foresight that Cheryl just didn't see. Maybe Ruthie knew that sooner or later Jimmy's free spirit was going to cause a strain on them building a real life together. Perhaps she could see that sooner or later Cheryl would bear the brunt of the marital weight and come to resent it. Perchance Ruthie could see that sooner or later the pressure of it all would be too much for either of them to take.

That was all in the past now and only pieces of their history together remained—the biggest piece being Yvonne. Somehow Cheryl had to muster up the courage to support what her daughter needed the most right now: a relationship with her father. Yet Cheryl's heart was waging a war of its own. She still loved Jimmy. She knew he needed help, but if she told anyone the type of help he really needed, he would likely spend the rest of his life locked away either in prison or in an asylum. Cheryl couldn't bear the thought of doing that to him, but she had to do something. Yvonne wanted to be around him, needed to be around him, but it wasn't safe. He wasn't safe. Jimmy needed help, and nothing Cheryl could do alone would ever be enough.

Cheryl looked for Ruthie and found her on the porch.

"Mama, you got a minute?" Cheryl asked Ruthie, who was

rocking in her cedar for the first time in nearly a week.

"Sure kiddo. What's up?"

"Our latest addition to the Boyd womanhood is what's up."

"My grandbaby? Then have a seat."

"Well, Mama, I'll cut to the chase. Yvonne wants her father at her birthday dinner on Sunday."

"Oh?"

"Yes. I know how you feel about Jimmy, but he's still her father. Things aren't copacetic between me and him right now, and I don't know when or if they'll ever be again," Cheryl said, letting out a deep sigh. "But what I do know is that Vonnie misses him, and it would mean the world to her to have him here on Sunday. I just want to know if you're okay with that."

"Sure. Who am I to stand in the way of a girl and her father?" Ruthie said calmly.

"Really? Just like that? No, I-told-you-sos or I-wouldn't-do-that-if-I-were-yous?"

"None at all. Besides, it's not my comfort that matters the most.

"Believe it or not, I'm still learning and growing, too. I've made my share of mistakes just like Jimmy. I've done some things in the past because I thought I was protecting people. Turns out I might have caused more harm than good. I know things between you and Jimmy aren't perfect, but find a way to work it out for Yvonne's sake, Cherylie-Bean."

"Mama, you haven't called me that in years."

"You're still my baby. I never want to cause you any pain. You're a good mother, Cheryl, so I know you feel that same way about my grandbaby. Her relationship with her father may not go smoothly all the time, but *sometimes*, something is better than nothing.

"Vonnie is strong and she's smart. I think, with your help and mine, she can glean whatever she can from her father—whatever little bit he can offer—and still turn out all right. Maybe it's time for her to see that people don't have to be perfect to love her or be loved by her. But to make it an easier pill for you to swallow, maybe we shouldn't have her party here."

"What, no Sunday dinner at the house? I'm surprised. What do you have in mind?"

"Someplace neutral is all," Ruthie said. "Just so the peace you've made for yourself here isn't shaken. We could probably use the fellowship hall down at the church."

"Mama, that's the last place I want to air my dirty laundry. All those nosy church folk, lingering around just to pry into my personal business."

"All right. All right. Point taken. Maybe I'll ask Mr. Pratt if the VA is available. He doesn't talk about it much, but I know he spends a lot of time volunteering down there. Perhaps he can get us in their hall for a few hours. I'll ask him about it."

"Thank you, Mama. That really means a lot."

"Cheryl. When are you going to tell me what happened so I can really help you?"

"Soon enough, Mama. Soon enough. But I will say this, you might stand by your original opinion of Jimmy once you find out what happened."

"I can't say that I won't be tempted to do that. But we've all made our share of mistakes, including me," Ruthie said, gently reaching for Cheryl's hand. "I pray you can remember that."

THE STORM

He's sweet, I know. He's sweet, I know.
Storm clouds may rise. Strong winds may blow.
But I'll tell the world,
Wherever I go,
That I have found a savior and He's sweet, I know.

Sunday service started with a rousing call and response from the Deacon Board of Bethesda Baptist Church. The tone was set for a worship that transcended the pains and struggles of the week before and brought hope for the new days ahead. A congregational song broke out and parishioners stood to their feet with shouts of praise.

"Church, today the Lord wants me to tell you that He may not always meet your needs immediately, but He will always meet your immediate needs," Reverend Falls said, preparing to take up a special collection. "We're starting Vacation Bible School next week and we need a little extra to cut the cost for all the children. So I want to encourage you to dig a little deeper today, please sir and please ma'am. The good Lord will make sure your needs are taken care of when you tend to the needs of others."

"Mama, can I go to Vacation Bible School?" Yvonne whispered to Cheryl.

"We'll have to see how much it costs. Someone kind of has a birthday celebration that took up most of my money today. We'll give it a try, though."

"I know some of you may still be giving," Reverend Falls continued, "but I want to jump right into this morning's lesson. My subject for today is 'Confronting Your Giants.'

"Most of us are familiar with the story of David and Goliath in the book of First Samuel. We know that this young shepherd boy was voted Least Likely to Succeed by his own family. We know this because when the prophet came to town to anoint a new king, David's father presented all of his sons for the job except David. Turns out David was the one God actually chose to anoint as the next king. But he didn't get his crown right away. People still had David running errands and tending to his father's sheep. But that all ended the day Goliath came to town.

"What we don't often talk about in this text is that the giant Goliath taunted the Israelites every day for forty long days. Goliath said they didn't have a soldier brave enough to fight him. Some of us have giants taunting us day after day, too. These giants are telling us we're not strong enough, smart enough, big enough, or good enough. These giants are in our present-day issues on our jobs, in our schools, and even in our homes. For some of us, our giants are calling out to us from our past, saying we'll never be free from the consequences of bad decisions, that no one will ever understand us or forgive us. So we get bullied into holding it all inside, day after day, month after month, and year after year.

"It's time for us to be like David and confront our giants once and for all. We need to stop running from them, hiding from them, and even ignoring them. Remember, saints, anything you run from will always keep chasin' ya.

"How good it must have felt to David to finally kill his giant! We need to kill our giants, too. No, I'm not talking about physically injuring someone or something. But I am saying it's time to kill our giants with the truth. A giant is just another word for the devil, and the Good Book tells us he's a liar and the father of lies! So what better way to kill a lie than to release the truth?

"It's time to throw the truth at your giant's head like David threw those smooth stones. It's time to hit your enemy smack-dab between his crooked eyes with every ounce of truth you can muster! Yes, the truth will defeat your enemy, but it will also make you free!

"Say it with me, church: And you shall know the truth," Reverend Falls started.

"And the truth shall make you free," echoed the congregation.

"So go get free from the guilt. Get free from the worry. Get free from the fear. Get free from the depression. Get free from the isolation! It's all a lie, and that giant's got to die!"

Reverend Falls's sermon came to a rousing close as people popped up from the pews to their feet with a round of applause and shouts of amen.

"Everyone please stand for the benediction," Reverend Falls said. "I pray for traveling grace upon you all and that in the coming week you know no hurt, harm, or danger."

Reverend Falls walked down the center aisle to complete his tradition of greeting Bethesda's members and visitors as they prepared to exit the double doors.

Ruthie embraced the members of the Willing Workers Committee and this time the Mothers Board, who would soon begin grooming her for membership. Dressed in a floral print dress, pink gloves, and a pink hat, she eventually maneuvered her way up the center aisle to Reverend Falls.

"Well, aren't you colorful today, Sister Ruthie."

"I had this ole thing tucked away in my closet, collecting dust. Just figured it was time to wear it, I guess."

"No need to explain wardrobes to me, Sister Ruthie. That's my wife's department," Reverend Falls said with a chuckle.

"Reverend, I must say that today's message was right on time for me," Ruthie said.

"Thank God that the message blessed you. I was in prayer last week and that's the scripture that came to me. I hope it was helpful to a lot of people."

"Oh, I'm sure it was, Reverend. You and First Lady Ida are still joining us this afternoon, right?"

"Wouldn't miss it for the world," he said.

"I let Mrs. Falls know we changed our location, on account of it being my grandbaby's birthday."

"Yes, she mentioned that this morning. By the way, you never told me all the details of what you need to say to your family today. Whatever it is, we'll be there for support."

"I truly thank you, Reverend Falls. I truly do."

"Granny, can JoAnne ride with us to the party?" Yvonne interrupted, having pushed her way up the reception line.

"Grandbaby, I wouldn't mind, but unfortunately we can't squeeze another soul into John's car. We're already a bit tight with Anne riding in the front seat with me."

"Miss Yvonne, the first lady and I will be sure to get JoAnne to your party in time for all the festivities," Reverend Falls added. "Plus that will give you all a little more time to set up without too many people being in the way."

"All right then, I guess," Yvonne said. "Thank you."

Cheryl, Sheila, and Anne took staccato steps forward for their turn to greet the pastor. Cheryl shied back a bit as if the physical distance would help Reverend Falls forget their last confrontation. Sheila hoped the man of the cloth couldn't somehow discern her whereabouts over the past week. There were no sunglasses to hide their faces there, only knee-length skirts and church-worthy blouses.

All niceties exchanged, the Boyd women descended the stairs

of Bethesda and walked toward John's car, which was already parked out front. They took no extra time for conversation as final preparations were needed to celebrate the newest woman in the clan.

The Boyds made a quick stop home before heading over to the hall, just long enough to gather the food and decorations for the party. On the dinner menu were Sunday staples: smothered chicken, fried white potatoes, succotash, Parker House rolls, and, for dessert, Yvonne's caramel birthday cake and chocolate chip cookies. There was an excitement as Yvonne's birthday celebration would be an official rite of passage for her to join the adult conversation table. There was also an undercurrent of anxiety, as each of the Boyd women warred with thoughts of how to deal with their own secret giants.

John dropped them off at the hall, helped unload supplies, and gave Cheryl a nod that he was on the way to pick up Jimmy.

"I'm gonna trust these womenfolk to you while I make a run," Jimmy said to Mr. Pratt, who had arrived early to greet them at the door.

"Yes, sir. They're about as safe here with these old vets as any place on the whole South Side. Let me grab some of these bags for you, ladies."

Yvonne was the first through the threshold wearing a new sunny yellow summer dress and a fresh coat of the pink lip gloss Cheryl had bought for her special day. Sheila and Anne took to decorating, intertwining pink and yellow streamers to mount around the walls. Yvonne's friend Thelma arrived just in time to blow up thirteen balloons.

Ruthie tended to the food and table settings. She saw no use in letting a good home-cooked meal go without a decent display. She had already brought over her good set of everyday plates, and now took to trying to honor a Boyd family tradition.

"Mr. Pratt, could I trouble you for some real glasses?"

"Glasses? Yes, ma'am. But, you know, we have plenty of paper cups. Easier on the cleanup."

"No paper for a young woman like Yvonne. Not today. Only the real deal."

"Yes, Ms. Ruthie. Right away."

True, the Boyds restrained children from glassware out of the likelihood of breakage. It was a sign of maturity and poise when they were deemed worthy to use a real glass. Yet this time, it meant even more. Ruthie wanted Yvonne to go into her womanhood with a clear view of what she was drinking in, taking into her life. Ruthie wanted her to learn from day one to make her decisions based on all she could see, nothing hidden, no mistaken perceptions, no fear-filled agendas. The glassware was Ruthie's wish for Yvonne to have a life full of clarity, purity, and strength.

Ruthie got lost in the extra décor details to keep her mind off the nervous tension brewing in the pit of her belly. The sound of new voices echoing through the beige-painted hall broke her focus.

"Oh, Reverend, First Lady, come right on in," Ruthie said. "Make yourselves comfortable while I finish dressing the table."

"Let me help you," Ida said.

"No, you're our guest."

"But I insist," Ida petitioned. "I always feel at home around you all, Sister Boyd. Please allow me to help you."

"Well then, no sense twisting my arm. Come right this way," Ruthie said, smiling and directing Ida to the table. "JoAnne, you can go find the guest of honor. No telling where she wandered off to in a place like this. Reverend Falls, feel free to have a seat."

"With all the war memorabilia around here? No way," he said, gazing at the tributes to the wars gone by in old framed photos scattered along the walls and glass-enclosed medals.

"My husband thinks he's a history buff," Ida said jokingly.

Cheryl was off in her own world, quietly piddling around. She was desperately looking for anything to calm her bubbling anxiety about seeing Jimmy for the first time since moving back home. Her breaths were short and tight, her shoulders locked and braced for sudden impact.

Cheryl tried her best to keep her back to the door, hoping to drag out the exact moment when she would again stand face-to-face with Jimmy. She slowly moved toward the record player and asked Ida if she and the right reverend would be offended by a little Stevie Wonder. Having received her blessing, Cheryl placed the LP on the turntable. She intentionally kept the volume at a minimum.

Suddenly there was a creaking sound at the door. John had returned with Papa Boyd, who decided to venture out on account of the meal rather than the company, and the infamous special guest.

"Well, everybody, look what the wind blew in," John announced. "It's Jimmy!"

Jimmy stood frozen beside John, hands by his sides, stiff at attention. He was unsure of where to place his feet next. His steps were delicate, as if he had just entered a room that was booby-trapped with hand grenades. He had cleaned up a bit since the last time anyone had seen him. He was shaven, Afro neatly groomed, and wearing clean jeans and a pressed short-sleeved dashiki. It was obvious that John had taken extra time to help Jimmy look presentable before his baby girl.

Reverend Falls walked over to greet him with a hearty handshake. Sheila immediately embraced her long-lost brother-in-law.

"It's been too long since I've seen you, brother," Sheila said. "How have you been?"

"I've been hanging tough, Lil' Sis," Jimmy replied.

An awkward pause entered the flow of conversation as Jimmy and Cheryl's eyes connected for the first time.

"Hey there, Cheryl," Jimmy said, trying to keep his voice from showing his nervousness.

"Hey there yourself," Cheryl replied mildly.

"Well, I'm happy to have all of my family and friends under the same roof," Ruthie interjected to pick up the conversation. "It's always such a blessing when we can all come together like this."

"Family is the most important thing," Ida said. "It just makes the rest of the craziness in the world seem more bearable."

"Let me check on Papa Boyd and the food," Ruthie said. "We should be about ready to eat."

John and Jimmy began slowly walking in, following the Reverend Falls's self-proclaimed tour through the photos he had already seen.

"I hear a familiar voice," Cheryl said. "Sounds like the birthday girl is about to make her grand entrance. And here she is now."

"Hi, everybody . . . Daddy!" Yvonne ran past everyone else and melted into her father's arms. "Daddy, you came! You came."

"I wouldn't miss this for the whole world, Vonnie," Jimmy said, still embracing her. Reaching into his pocket, he pulled out a small package wrapped in comic strip paper. "I got you a little something. You can see it later when you open up your gifts."

"Thanks, Daddy!"

"That's righteous, man," John said. "Vonnie, they always say good things come in small packages. You just might have the key to the city in there."

"I hope it is the key to the city," Sheila said. "Maybe my niece can use her clout to get me free CTA bus rides for a year."

"If that's the key to the city, maybe Yvonne can finally get me a meeting with the mayor," Reverend Falls added jokingly.

"Yvonne, let me take your gift for you," Cheryl said. "I'll put it with your other gifts."

"She already has my gift," Sheila said. "Don't you, Vonnie?"

"Yep! I sure do."

"So what did your Auntie Sheila get you?" Jimmy asked.

"She gave me a diary."

"A diary? Aren't you a little young to be keeping things all to yourself?" Jimmy asked.

"I thought the same thing," Cheryl said to Jimmy. "But then I realized she needed an outlet, too. Plus, she found out that she likes to write poetry."

"You like poems do you?" Jimmy said. "Sounds like you might have the art bug like your daddy."

"She has a lot of your ways, Jimmy," Cheryl added.

"I hope they're all the good ones," Jimmy said somberly.

"Yes, the good ones."

"Okay, everyone, dinner is served," Ruthie announced, pointing to the buffet spread along a side table. "Everyone, get a plate and then come grab a seat. Yvonne, you sit on this side between your mom and dad."

"Looks like today's your big day, Vonnie," Cheryl said as Jimmy helped Yvonne pull out her chair at the big people's table.

After a few moments of chatter, the buffet line dwindled and everyone was seated.

"Well, everyone, today my grandbaby Yvonne turns thirteen years old," Ruthie announced to a roomful of clapping and cheers. "In the Boyd family, we have a tradition of graduating our young from the kiddie table to the big people's table when they turn thirteen. They get to drink out of real glasses and hear the things that we adults converse about around the dinner table. It's our way of welcoming them into the next stage of their lives and saying that we recognize the maturity and growth in them. Today it's Yvonne's turn. And I must say that as this family's matriarch, I couldn't be prouder of the strong young lady she's growing up to be. Here's to Yvonne."

Everyone raised their glasses of lemonade in honor of Yvonne's rite of passage into young adulthood. Reverend Falls said grace over the food and conversation.

Dinner conversation was jovial as the focus of the meal remained on the one person they all had as a common denominator: Yvonne. Stevie was crooning *You Are the Sunshine of My Life*.

After a chorus of *Happy Birthday* and cake and cookies for dessert, Ruthie knew it was time to wash one last load of emotional laundry.

"John, would you mind turning down the music some?" she said.

"Mama, I already have the volume down low," Cheryl remarked, pausing between bites of cake.

"I know. It's just that I have something important to say and I want everyone to hear me."

"Okay, Mama," John said, looking at Ruthie with compassion. He knew that what she was about to say was probably the hardest thing she would ever say, but also the most freeing.

"I, um—I just first want to thank Reverend Falls and the first lady for coming to be with us on today. I called him up this past week and said I had some news to share with the family, and that I really would like their support."

"Mama, you're scaring me. Are you sick?" Sheila asked.

"No. No, Shay. Nothing like that. I, uh—well, let's just say that the reverend's sermon today couldn't have come at a more perfect time. I have a giant of my own—a giant secret that I've been keeping for years. It wasn't right for me to keep it, but at the time it made sense to.

"I wanna just say how much I love all of my children, and that I would never do anything to purposely hurt you or put you in harm's way. I just made a bad call in my decisions, and I never found the right time to make things right again."

"Mama, what are you talking about?" Cheryl pressed.

Ruthie began rubbing her hands repeatedly back and forth on her lap. She was instinctively trying to soothe away the waves of pain as they came crashing to the surface from her past. Her gaze dropped to the empty plate before her. She had inwardly regressed to the insecure nineteen-year-old she'd once been.

Reverend Falls could see that Ruthie was unnerved in a way he had never witnessed before. He stood and placed his hand on her right shoulder for support; Ida grabbed hold of Ruthie's left.

"The other day, John brought something to my attention that I had tried so hard to forget. He said that he was rummaging around in the basement for some old records and came across . . . a trunk. Turns out it was my most prized possession—my mother's old trunk. I got it from her some years back when you all were still little kids. I stored it in the darkest, smallest part of the basement because I knew my three children were too afraid to go back there. I forgot about it. I also forgot that one day my babies would grow up, and maybe not be so afraid of the unknown anymore.

"Well." She paused to swallow. "In that trunk is a crate filled with old pictures and memories from my high school days. My diploma's in there, and so are a bunch of letters."

"John, is this the same crate of pictures you showed me the other day?" Cheryl asked.

"Uh . . . yeah, it is, Sis," John replied.

"Cheryl, John told me you saw a picture of me with a young man in uniform the same year you were born. It wasn't Papa Boyd."

"Yeah, I noticed. John and I even joked about it a little bit. I figured you had some secret sweetheart that you never told us about," Cheryl said.

"Yes, I did. And, um, Cheryl . . . that man is your father."

Cheryl's fork stopped in midair. Then it crashed to her plate as her right hand grew numb. Her eyes were fixed on her cake, which had immediately become the contradictory sweet backdrop to the bitter words she was now hearing from Ruthie's mouth. It seemed to her that everyone seated around her had gone mute. Ruthie's words became muffled in Cheryl's ears.

"Baby, I never meant to hurt you. I never wanted to hurt you. Please believe me." Ruthie took a deep breath. "Your Papa didn't, either. If you want to be mad at someone, be mad at me. He always wanted to tell you, but I thought it would just cause too much confusion in the home.

"I had no way of telling you anything about your father anyway 'cause I—I just cut him out of our lives. I thought it would be easier this way."

"Yvonne, maybe you and your friends should excuse yourselves from the table now," Ida interrupted, hoping to shield their innocence and preserve Ruthie's dignity in their eyes.

"With all due respect, First Lady," Ruthie said, "that won't be necessary this time. There have been enough secrets for long enough. I tried to shield Cheryl so much when she was younger that I did her more harm than good. I don't want that for my grandbaby. The others can leave, but Yvonne, you're strong enough to take this. You're so much like me."

"Papa, is this true?" Her voice cracking with every syllable.

"Yeah, baby, it's true. Your mama thought it was best not to tell you. So I didn't say nothing more about it," Papa Boyd said. "I took care of you just the same."

"Your father was a good man, a navy man," Ruthie continued. "He wanted to take care of us, but I was just too young and scared to see it. I met your papa and we soon got married. So I—I just decided to start us off with a clean slate. No ties to the past. No regrets.

"I originally planned to only keep things from you a little while, just when you were a baby," Ruthie said. "Then I thought it would be better if I waited until you got through your childhood, for your self-esteem. Then, a little while meant waiting until you finished high school. Then time flew by, and before I knew it, you were grown with a family of your own. It seemed like the right time to tell you, Cheryl, was gone."

"Then why say something to me now?" Cheryl charged in an interrogating tone.

"I read the letters, Cheryl," John said. "I found out the truth. And after I had already made the mistake of letting you know about the letters in the first place, I just couldn't keep it from you. And I didn't think Mama should either. I thought it had been a secret long enough. It wasn't good for you to be in the dark, and it wasn't healthy for Mama."

"So, that's it?" Cheryl pushed away from the table, threw up her hands in disgust, and leaped to her feet.

"That's how this goes? People just decide to hold back half my damn life from me, and think that's okay? Then in one instant, poof! It's time to tell Cheryl! It's time to tell Cheryl!"

"Sister Cheryl, please try to calm down," Reverend Falls said.

"When is this ever gonna be *my* life?" Cheryl said, screaming at the top of her voice. "When will I ever be in the driver's seat? Huh, Reverend? Will someone please tell me that?

"All this time I thought you were trying to keep Shay from turning out to be like me, and it was you all along!"

Cheryl's tears were uncontrollable. Yvonne was frozen to her seat and torn between the emotions of two women she adored. Jimmy temporarily lapsed into his role of protector and stood to comfort his wife. Cheryl was too weak to even flinch away from his touch.

"You're a hypocrite, Mama," Sheila added. "I can't believe Perfect Patty messed up, too. You're always riding my back, and look at you!"

"Look, I'm still the mother here! I didn't put those thoughts in either one of your heads, let alone those ugly words in your mouths. I raised you both the best way I knew how so you wouldn't repeat my mistakes! I tried to be a better example. What you did with that is between you and the Lord!"

"Can we all just calm down here?" Reverend Falls said, trying to regain peace in the conversation. "Let's all have a seat. Please!"

Cheryl took in a deep breath and slumped back down into her chair.

"If I had known all this would happen, I would've just kept my mouth shut and the box to myself," John said sternly.

"But what good would that have done, John?" Reverend Falls asked. "That would have been yet another layer on a festering sore that was bound to boil over someday. Now at least it's out in the open air and can breathe so it can heal.

"I know this is a very emotional moment for everyone," he went on. "It's never easy to hear something like this. But y'all can't be at each other's throats like we're in a war zone. I know this is a veteran's hall, but the firing squad has got to go.

"Cheryl, I pray that once the shock of this wears off, you can really hear your mother's heart. She was basically still a girl when she had you. She didn't know how else to take care of you. I'm not making excuses for anyone, but I believe she did the best she could.

"And Sister Ruthie, I commend you for being brave enough to tell your daughter the truth. Yes, your decisions hurt you and they hurt Cheryl. But you killed that giant today. Now that hurt doesn't get to be a lasting scarlet letter on your chest or hers. The harm gets lifted when we expose the lie and tell the truth, y'all."

"I've been through a lot, Reverend," Ruthie said, the pain audible in her voice, "and the half of it ain't been told here today. My father used to beat us so bad, till I was afraid to live at home with Cheryl. I didn't want him touching my baby. I couldn't afford a place of my own, so I had to take my baby girl to live in a tiny kitchenette with three other families.

"I was scraping by and only made seven dollars a week—only seven dollars a week," Ruthie said solemnly as a single tear slowly began to flow. "Somehow I'm still here, though. After every hurt, heartbreak, heartache, I'm still here. Even with tears in my eyes, I'm still here.

"With all that I've been through, I had the nerve to keep moving. I had the nerve to keep getting back up for more. Like the first batch of pain wasn't good enough. I kept bouncing back.

"I even surprised myself. I kept thinking, woman when will enough be enough for you? Why won't you just shrivel up and die?"

"Sister Ruthie," Ida said quietly, "you just reminded me about Job. Anytime I used to hear the story of Job, I'd blame his wife for telling him to curse God and die. I couldn't understand how anyone could ever feel so low that they'd want to curse the very God who made them. But then I had some of those days for myself, and then I thought sister girl Mrs. Job knew a little something.

"There have been times I had questions, too," Ida said. "How could I trust a Man who allowed me to feel some of the deepest cuts? How could I love Someone who left me wide open to hurt? Then I'd say, how couldn't I? How couldn't I trust the One who knows everybody's hurts, but thinks enough of me not to snuff me out for complaining about mine? How could I complain about a God who catches every tear and turns my sorrows into joy—even if it's in His own time?

"Yes, you all are hurting right now. I can't lie and say you're not. But in the whole scheme of things, there's no real harm done," Ida said. "None that your love for one another and the Lord above can't handle."

"I know what you're saying is true," Ruthie said. "I just have to choose not to let my burdens get so heavy that I forget to breathe. You know, that's why they say people get so worn out when they're running a race, because they forget to breathe."

"God is breath," Ida said. "That's the way I see it; and if I keep taking Him in, then all the bad air eventually has to leave."

"What's his name?" Cheryl asked Ruthie.

"Your father? Your father's name is Monroe Jackson."

"Cheryl, I'll try to find him for you if you want to meet him," John said quietly. "I think there are enough clues in the letters about where to start."

"I could always reach out to my old friend Earnestine," Ruthie added. "Her husband Tommy had contact with him off and on through the years. We could start there."

"I—I don't think I'm ready for any of that. This is all so sudden."

"I understand, Cheryl," Ruthie said. "There's no pressure on you whatsoever. I'm sorry, Cheryl, for everything."

Holding back tears, Ruthie turned to the youngest woman of her offspring.

"Grandbaby, I hate that you had to hear all this on your birthday. I just hope you learn from Granny's mistakes. It's not always good to keep things from the ones you love, even if you think you're helping them in the long run. Being hurt is one thing. The harm

164

comes in when we try to sweep things under the rug. I don't want to harm anyone anymore.

"So . . . I guess I've done enough emotional spring cleaning for the next few years. If anyone else has any secrets, I suggest you do like the good reverend said in his message today and confront your giant. Let's put it all on the table and trust that we have enough love toward one another to get past it."

"Granny?"

"Yes, Grandbaby?"

"I've got a secret," Yvonne said. "Well, sort of. I told Mama already, but I didn't tell the person it was about." She turned to look her aunt in the eye. "Auntie Sheila—"

"No, baby," Cheryl interrupted, "you don't have to tell her anything. She already knows."

"She knows that Thelma and I saw Bobby kiss another woman outside the laundromat?"

"I do now," Sheila said dejectedly, turning to Cheryl. "How long did you know, Cheryl?"

"I only found out just a few days before you did, Sis. I wanted to tell you, I just didn't know how. I didn't know if you'd believe me. Plus, I didn't want to place any of that burden on Vonnie. She's still my baby and she shouldn't have to be placed in the middle of something like that."

"I get that, Cheryl. But *you* knew! You knew!" Sheila burst into tears. "You knew I looked like a fool and you didn't tell me."

"Now, wait a minute, Sheila," Reverend Falls interjected. "I don't know the details here, but seems to me that Cheryl had your best interest at heart, too."

"Auntie Shay, I made her promise not to tell," Yvonne admitted. "I didn't want to hurt your feelings. I wanted it not to be true."

"Out of the mouths of babes," Reverend Falls said. "I think that's at the heart of everything I've heard here today. People have sworn themselves and even others to secrecy thinking that they were protecting somebody else. You each were thinking that if you ignored the trouble, maybe it would just go away. But life doesn't work that way."

"You're right," Sheila said, whimpering. "I've been keeping a secret of my own, and I made Cheryl promise not to tell anyone, too. Mama," she said, now crying even harder. "You were right, and I was too embarrassed to admit it."

"Admit what, Shay?" Ruthie asked, just above a whisper.

"Robert was wrong, all wrong. He's married and I didn't even know it! I didn't find out until I thought I was pregnant. I'm so ashamed."

"Oh my God, Shay," Ruthie said.

"I was too stupid to even see it. And Cheryl, you're right. I probably wouldn't have believed you if you'd told me first."

A reflective moment of silence rested on the now dismal battlefield. The weaponry of words had been dismantled like an empty gun.

"Sheila," Ida said, "I had a similar situation happen to me when I was about your age. I was in college and thought I knew everything. I fell in love with my teacher's aide. He was in grad school and I thought he was the cat's meow. Turned out he was married with a two-year-old son. I was devastated. I felt dirty, stupid, humiliated. But eventually I realized that I'm not my mistakes, but the product of my decisions. I got myself back up, dusted myself off, and started my life over again. I looked at the bright side, and you should too—it could've been worse."

Cheryl felt anxious and nervous inside. The presence of truth was a pressure within itself. It had a way of forcing everything hidden to the surface, and she too felt its power overtaking her. Cheryl was trying not to break under its control, feeling that her staunch stance was strength in itself. Truth or dare. Truth or consequences. All her childhood games were now ingrained in her adult psyche. She lived by their rules: the one who told the truth first was weak, and the one who held their ground longest was strong. Would she teach Yvonne to live by the same rules? The pressure built even more on Cheryl's chest. Her emotional airflow was constricted. She had to take in a fresh breath. The greater power would win.

"Since we're all telling secrets here, I'd like to share mine," Cheryl began. "Jimmy, I still love you, but the truth is I'm afraid to be near you." She looked around the room. "I never told anyone about the night I came back home to Mama's, and I don't even think Jimmy remembers.

"He'd been out late, drinking and only God knows what else. Anne had come over to stay the weekend with Yvonne. It was really late, so the two of them had fallen off to sleep. So had I, but I heard him when he came into the apartment."

Jimmy turned his head in Cheryl's direction, but never lifted his eyes.

"He came into the bedroom, bumping into things. He kept asking me for his silver buttons, his silver buttons. I had no idea what he meant. I guess I must have agitated him because something went off inside of him, like he wasn't there anymore. He started talking about his lieutenant and how he wasn't going to let him set him up to die like the man did to his boot camp buddy.

"I kept trying to calm him down, to get him to come to bed, but he wouldn't. He started getting louder. The only reason he didn't wake the girls was because it was thundering like crazy that night. Jimmy opened up the window and started screaming and crying. I didn't know what to do. Somehow I finally I got him to lie down.

"We both fell off to sleep, or at least I thought he was asleep. I don't know what went wrong inside of him, but I woke up an hour later with a gun to my head. He dragged me up on my knees and knelt behind me like I was a prisoner of war and said he would kill me."

Cheryl took panting breaths between her words as if she needed to come up for air after each syllable. Her palms were sweating. Her mouth was dry. She could hear the claps of thunder all over again. One after the other. Louder and louder. Yet it was the click of Jimmy's .38 Special that echoed through her mind. The pressure of the cold, hard steel against her brow.

"Yvonne must have heard me crying because she opened the door and turned on the light. I—I panicked. I didn't want her to see me or her father that way. I told her to go to our neighbor for help. I didn't want anyone to call the cops or an ambulance. I didn't want to trigger him with sirens.

"I think when Jimmy saw Yvonne, he somehow came to himself. It was like a miracle happened because he let me go, and he dropped the gun. I took off running and I didn't look back.

"I eventually told Yvonne to forget what she saw, that it never happened, to keep it just between us. I made her promise not to tell. I bought my baby into that lie so much that she doesn't even remember what really happened."

Jimmy's head dropped to his chest. He was fighting to hold back the tears. He had no words to explain the actions of the man even he no longer knew.

The others could feel the heaviness of that night in the room. Yvonne began to cry, trying so hard not to reconcile her mother's story with her own scattered memories. Ruthie found the strength once again to slowly stand and walk to her daughter's side. Cheryl's face was streaming with tears. It was worn from the battle of trying to hold on to a lie.

"Jimmy," Cheryl said. "I'm not bringing this up to cause you any trouble. I've kept quiet because I don't want you to get hurt. But it's been killing me inside to hold all this in. I love you, but you need help, Jimmy—real help. And until and unless you do that, there's never gonna be another chance for us.

"Yvonne, I know you love your father. So I promise to do whatever I can to help you two stay close. But I can't promise it will all work out the way you want it to, baby. I'm so sorry."

The room grew still. Truth had frozen them all in their tracks. The only sound was the rustle of Mr. Pratt opening his suitcoat to retrieve a single item from his inside breast pocket.

"Mr. Jimmy," Mr. Pratt said. "I know we don't know each other well, but I was always taught to never leave a fellow soldier down. Please take this. I want you to have it."

The two men firmly locked hands across the table. The exchange was simple, yet poignant. It was Mr. Pratt's ten-year sobriety medallion.

"I don't like to talk about it much, but I lost my wife and my daughter in a house fire," Mr. Pratt said. "Folks down South speculated on how the fire got started, but I knew. Me and my family desegregated a block and some folks didn't like it.

"I survived Korea, active duty no less. I saw some God-awful things over there, but nothing shook me like when I lost my wife and child. It sent me to a place so dark I couldn't get back on my own. I started using heroin to numb the pain. Then I needed it just to make it through the day. Before I knew it, I'd lost everything else I had left. That was until someone shone a light back on my soul, Mr. Jimmy. I'm not myself again. Don't know if I'll ever be, but I'm at peace. Let me help you find your peace, Mr. Jimmy."

Mr. Pratt tightened his hold on Jimmy's hand. His grip felt like a lifeline to Jimmy as he began sobbing freely.

RAIN AND RAINBOWS

The remainder of Yvonne's birthday was spent in a profound silence in the Boyd home. Everyone was off in their separate corners, hoping to somehow regain their composure or at least find a new way to live in their truth.

Ruthie was seated, hands clasped in prayer, at her dining room table. The evening gospel radio broadcast was crooning softly in the background. An afternoon rain shower left a cool breeze that was slowly blowing through an open window. Ruthie, like the others, was in deep thought, replaying what she had said and what she had heard, praying within herself for an answer.

"Ms. Ruthie. Ms. Ruthie?"

"Oh! Um, yes, Mr. Pratt? What can I do for you?"

"I just came down for an evening cup of coffee," he said, holding his own cup with both hands. "I figure, with all that went on today, a second cup of caffeine might do me some good."

"Go right ahead. Help yourself."

Mr. Pratt slipped into the kitchen and poured his coffee with military precision, adding just enough sugar. He reemerged into Ruthie's presence.

"Ms. Ruthie?"

"Yes, Mr. Pratt?"

"I've been thinking about what happened at the VA today. I feel terrible about things. I hope it works out somehow."

"Me, too."

"Ms. Ruthie?"

"Yes, Mr. Pratt?"

"What did you say was the name of your old fella again?"

"Who? Cheryl's father?" Ruthie asked mildly.

"Yes, Ms. Ruthie," Mr. Pratt said, cradling his cup.

"Monroe. Monroe Jackson. Why do you ask?"

"Name's familiar, that's all."

"Familiar?"

"Yes, ma'am. One of the fellas down at the VA . . . never mind."

"One of the fellas, what?"

"One of the fellas down at the VA has the same name is all. Maybe it's just coincidence, but the Monroe Jackson I know was a navy man, too. Originally from right here. He stays in Gary, Indiana, now, but he comes into the city once a week to volunteer."

"I'm sorry to disturb you, Ms. Ruthie. I'll be getting out of your way," Mr. Pratt said, quickly pivoting to leave the room.

"No, wait!" Ruthie said, finally managing to push words out of her mouth since hearing Mr. Pratt's serendipitous discovery. "You know Monroe?"

"Sure I do. Well, I know a Monroe. Who knows if it's the same one?"

"But it could be. I can't believe it," she said with a dumbfounded tone. "After all this time. He could have been just one person away from me after all this time?"

"Ms. Ruthie, don't go getting your hopes up. I can ask about him tomorrow is all. Only if you want me to. I don't want to pry."

"Please! Please ask. Maybe it's time for everything to finally come full circle." Her eyes brightened. "Here, take this."

Ruthie reached into her housecoat pocket for an item she had been carrying around for the past week. It was a wallet-sized photo of Monroe in his naval uniform. A handwritten inscription on the back read, "To my heart and soul, Ruthie. Love always, Monroe."

"If it's the same Monroe, he's sure to recognize himself."

"Ms. Ruthie, I must say the resemblance is striking. Can't be sure just yet, but I'll ask first thing tomorrow."

"Thank you. Thank you so much."

Ruthie gently touched Mr. Pratt's forearm as if reaching out for a lifeline of her own. Could the missing piece to her puzzled memories and checkered realities have been this close to her all along?

* * *

The next morning, Ruthie was up early to wish Mr. Pratt well in his pursuit. She also wanted to confirm that their conversation the night before was not something she had dreamed. She sat back down in her dining room chair, glued to it as if being there would reconnect her tangible proof of Mr. Pratt's words. She replayed them in her mind over and over: "Ms. Ruthie, I must say the resemblance is striking."

The sound of keys clinked at the back door. It was John coming in from a night shift at the bus depot. Smelling the aroma of Folgers, he knew Ruthie was already awake. He braced himself for the certain aftershocks of the earthquake he had caused. Originally, it had all seemed like a good idea—pushing Ruthie into her truth. Noble, even. He'd just never envisioned the whole family coming undone.

"Morning, Mama," John said, treading lightly.

"Good morning yourself."

"How are you?"

"How do you think I am, John?"

"Sorry, Mama. I never meant for things to go like they did."

"So how did you think they would go? As street-smart as you can be, it never ceases to amaze me how truly naive you are. There was no way things were going to go any other way than they did."

"I just thought it was too important to keep a secret any longer. Too much damage was being done."

"You know what? You never think. That's the problem. You never think about anyone but yourself. You practically held me hostage to do what you wanted done."

"It wasn't like that, Mama."

"Yes, it was."

"I didn't mean to make you feel trapped."

"I think you did when you said either I had to tell Cheryl or you would do it yourself. That's plain English to me, Son. But you know what? I shouldn't even be angry with you at all. It was time for it all to be said and done. It was bound to all fall apart one day. You just happened to be the one to push over the first domino."

John always had to have the last word with Ruthie. He'd often been scolded for it while growing up. Yet he used those verbal sparring matches as the training ground for his greatest debates. He considered Ruthie's indiscretion his championship round. He had to make her see things fully this time, not through the eyes of a disciplinarian of children, but as an example before still-impressionable adults.

"I thought I was doing a solid thing, for you and for Cheryl.

Heck, for the whole family. Cheryl's 'round here darn near falling apart, Shay doesn't half the time know who she is, and Papa sits around all day like some zombie. I didn't mean for anyone to get hurt. I meant for things to get better. Somebody had to tell the truth around here, Mama. Why not you?"

"Why not who?" Cheryl had emerged for the day on the tail end of their conversation.

"I'm trying to make Mama see that she had to tell you the truth. We all needed the truth," John said. "Mama, what you did was courageous. And you gave other people the courage to do the same thing. One day you'll thank me for all this."

"How are you, Cheryl? I know I put a lot on you yesterday," Ruthie said, deflecting from John. "I'm sorry. I just didn't have another choice."

"No. You thought you didn't have another choice. I was angry yesterday, and I'm still not over it. But I understand what it feels like to tell your daughter something—or not tell her—because you think you have no other choice.

"Honestly, though, I don't blame you, because then I'd have to blame myself. I've been a basket case all summer long, and right in front of Yvonne. If I make you out to be a horrible mother, then so am I.

"Maybe I should meet him. Might help me sort through some of the missing pieces in my life. I always felt like something was missing, but I never knew what."

Ruthie stared off into the distance, overcome by Cheryl's words of redemption. A single stream flowed from her left eye.

"Thank you, baby," Ruthie said, laying her hands across her healing heart. "Thank you."

***

A while later, and now dressed in a purple A-line dress, Ruthie headed down the crackled sidewalk of Lexington Lane. Her steps were slow and deliberate, milking each moment of her time alone. Midway to the park, however, she made an impulsive detour toward Cottage Grove. The VA office was somewhere along that street. She knew Mr. Pratt needed time to investigate, but she was suddenly driven by the possibility of being that close to her real daydreams.

The more she walked, the louder her thoughts became. Gradually, Ruthie's self-chatter grew into nervous verbalization.

"I wonder what he looks like. Wait, I'm the one. Will he even recognize me? I've changed so much. Oh, how I've changed. Wait. I'm married. Why do I even care?"

The thought of being face-to-face with her memories overwhelmed Ruthie's reality. She had never even thought about what Monroe was doing with his present life. She was content to remember him as he had been, young and accepting of the person she hoped to be—not the person she had become. What would he think of her now? Ruthie had never told Monroe goodbye in person. She had taken the cowardly way out and had instead spent her existence being courageous before everyone except the one who deserved it the most.

Why couldn't she have been bold enough to tell Monroe the truth? Why didn't she tell him how afraid she was to live at home with her parents until he returned? Why did she panic and marry Papa Boyd? The questions were racing through her mind faster than any streetcar she had ever ridden. Only her nineteen-year-old self knew the answers. The woman she had become was wiser, more rational, and would have advised her predecessor Truthie Ruthie to live up to her name. The truth would have changed everything for her and Cheryl, but that was day-old news. All she could do now was confront her past fears with her present reality.

Ruthie anxiously arrived at the VA hall, slowly opened the door, and crossed the threshold.

"Ma'am, you look lost. May I help you?"

"Oh yes. I'm looking for, um . . . Mr. Pratt. Is Mr. Pratt here?"

"Pratt? Of course. When is he not here? I can go get him from the back. Who should I say is calling?"

"Ruthie Boyd."

"Boyd?"

"Yes. Boyd."

The man stared intensely at Ruthie before going to retrieve Mr. Pratt. The two men returned a short while later.

"Ruthie? Is that you?" Monroe asked, his voice steady but still unsure.

"Monroe?"

"I wondered what this moment would feel like, finally seeing you again," he said, immediately embracing her. "How are you, Ruthie?"

"Nearly speechless."

"I've never known you to have a loss of words."

"I have now."

"No need to clam up on me. You were always able to speak your mind."

"Well, Ms. Ruthie," Mr. Pratt said, "I kept my promise. I told Mr. Monroe your story and showed him his picture. Seems you two could use a moment to talk. Please excuse me."

"Where are my manners? Please, have a seat," Monroe said, slightly touching her shoulder. "Ruthie Tucker. I mean, Boyd. It's been a long time."

Ruthie's movements were nearly robotic as she struggled to lay hold of the surreal moment. A chance mention of his name aloud had led her right to Monroe after all these years. He was slightly shorter than she remembered and graying a bit, no doubt subtle signs of aging, but his features were still distinguished and warm. Her hands tingled. Her heart fluttered. She was alive again.

"So, what are you thinking? What's popped into your head?"

"How sorry I am," she said, hanging her head. "I made such a mess of things. Everything. For everybody. And I never had the guts to face you."

"What happened to us, Ruthie? You just shut me out and disappeared. Next thing I knew, I was getting word that you went off and got married. Did I do something wrong? I always wondered if I did something wrong."

"No. It wasn't you. It was all on me. I was young and afraid. I made a rash decision."

"Do you regret it?"

"I regret a lot of things, but I made my bed hard so I have to lie in it."

"What were you afraid of, Ruthie? Was it me?"

"No. None of this was ever because of you. I hate that you felt that way. I was the one afraid. I was afraid of being by myself. Afraid of raising our little girl alone."

"But you knew I was coming back to you. I loved you, Ruthie. A part of me always will.

"Your family was right there, Ruthie. That's the only way I would have ever felt comfortable leaving your side. I knew you were safe."

"But that's just it. I wasn't safe. Home wasn't a safe place for me and our baby. My father beat us, Monroe, really bad."

"You never said anything about that, Ruthie. You never said a word. I never would have left you there. You could have stayed with my folks till I got back home. Why didn't you say something?"

"I don't know."

"No, that's not true. You do know. Tell the truth."

"I—I was ashamed. I didn't want you to think I wasn't the person you thought I was. I wanted to still feel special around you, not pitied."

"Pity? So all of this was about protecting your pride? I loved you. It was my job to protect you, and you took that away from me. You took that away from our daughter, too. I was messed up about all of that for a really long time. I didn't know if you had been seeing someone else the whole time or what."

"She wants to meet you, Monroe," Ruthie said, deflecting his words and her overwhelming pain.

"She does? Are you sure?"

"Well, she's open to the idea. Cheryl's the type that when she's open to something, you have to jump on it right away. Otherwise, she tends to be a bit guarded."

"Like her mother, I see."

The two continued talking past their pain until they began to reminisce about old friends and the day they met. They caught up on the here and now as well, Monroe sharing that he eventually married and raised a family of his own in Gary. Chicago held too many memories, he explained. He'd never kept Cheryl a secret from his wife, he had just managed to move on. A few hours passed before either of them knew it.

"Listen, the hall is hosting a barbecue Saturday for Labor Day weekend. We give out school supplies for kids and talk about our services for vets. It's neutral territory. I'd love to see Cheryl. That is, if you think it's not too soon.

"You can bring the whole family. I wouldn't want your mister to have the wrong idea about us. All I really want is to still be friends. Maybe we can."

"I'd like that a lot. It may take some coaxing, but I'll give it a try."

"Ms. Ruthie," Mr. Pratt broke in gently. "I'm getting ready to head out for the day. Would you care for an escort home, or will you be staying longer?"

"Mr. Pratt, that's perfect timing. I've long overstayed my welcome."

"Never," Monroe said. "Hope to see you soon."

Ruthie and Mr. Pratt walked in silence. The day's developments had been too overwhelming for either of them to reconstruct. Ruthie rehearsed her pitch in her mind. She would tell the Boyds that it was high time they walked in their truth. No more secrets. Only liberty. The first task was introducing Cheryl to Monroe. It was a perfect idea to invite the family. That way no suspicions could arise and no one would feel ignored.

Ruthie got home and went straight to the kitchen. Her intention was to bring up Monroe's offer over dinner.

"Everyone, I have an announcement to make," Ruthie said. "We've been invited to a barbecue Saturday."

"Oh, really," Cheryl said. "Where?"

"Back at the VA."

"I don't know if I ever want to go back in there again," Sheila said.

"It's not the VA that caused our confusion. I did. We all did," Ruthie said. "Maybe we can go back and replace those memories."

"How, Granny?" Yvonne asked.

"Yeah, replace them with what?" John asked.

"Well, turns out that Mr. Pratt knew a Monroe Jackson down at the VA. We found your father, Cheryl," Ruthie said, eyes focused straight on Cheryl. "He'd like to meet you. He wants to meet *all* of you. You too, Papa.

"I know this is a lot to take in. But I think it will be good for all of us," she said. "John, don't you agree?"

"You know what? I do."

"I don't know about all of this, Mama," Cheryl said. "I don't think I'm ready. What about Papa? How does he feel about this?"

"Well, Papa? Your daughter wants to know how you feel," Ruthie said. "Will you go?"

"Yes, I'll go," Papa Boyd said. "Maybe it'll do some good to see what's been between us all these years."

Ruthie knew Papa Boyd had the final say. There was no further discussion needed. She spent the following days brooding over her flock, tending to even their unspoken needs to minimize any interference to their second chance—her second chance.

By Saturday, John had taken on Ruthie's excitement and even took it upon himself to invite Jimmy. After all, he was a veteran in need of VA services. Plus, it was another opportunity for Jimmy to see Yvonne without disturbing Cheryl too much.

"Hey, everybody, I'll drive Shay, Yvonne, and Mr. Pratt over first. Then I'll come back for the rest of you."

"Sounds good," Ruthie said, seated next to Cheryl in her rocking chair. "We're ready when you are."

"Cheryl?"

"Yes, Mama?"

"Are you all right?"

"About as all right as I can be."

"Cheryl, I'm not expecting you to start a relationship with him or anything. I'm just glad you're willing to meet him. I just feel like if you at least meet him, part of my wrongs to you can be made right. There's a chance for us to get some closure on all of this or maybe even start a new chapter."

"I'll meet him, but beyond that I don't know what I'll do. I've been thinking and thinking, until I just stopped thinking. Papa and I may not be the closest, but that's what I know. I don't know this Monroe character."

"I know you don't, but you have a lot of his ways."

"Really?"

"Yes. You're free-spirited like he is for sure. Clever, too."

"Hmm."

"Yep."

"Thank you for forgiving me, Cheryl, even before I asked. You just don't know how much that means to me."

"I kinda do."

"Yeah?"

"Yeah. I've had a few talks with Vonnie over the past couple weeks. I didn't know where to start. I couldn't apologize for feeling broken. But I wanted to apologize for making her feel broken, too. I couldn't seem to find the words, but wouldn't you know it, she did."

"What did she say?"

"First she told me, 'Daddy matters to me because I see myself through his eyes.' Then she said, 'Mama, you don't have to apologize for being human. I just want you honest and well.' That little thirteen-year-old broke me down with three words: honest and well."

"Sounds like my grandbaby, all right. It's the honest truth that makes us free. And who do you know that can be free but not well? The two just go together."

"I guess."

John pulled up in front of the house, ready to drive Ruthie, Cheryl, and Papa Boyd to the VA hall.

Ruthie stood and walked over to the doorway, calling out for Papa Boyd.

"Papa, John's back for us."

Papa Boyd slowly walked to the door.

"I changed my mind," he said. "We all have ghosts we need to face alone."

"Fine. Have it your way. You always do. I'll be back in time for dinner."

* * *

John parked, and Ruthie and Cheryl cautiously exited the El Dorado. People were gathered on the grassy lot adjacent to the hall. It was a festive and sunny day, the crowd peppered with old military berets and retired camouflage. Sheila had managed to find her second wind and was engaged in a giddy conversation with a young army recruiter. Cheryl immediately spotted Yvonne with Jimmy, and looked at John with discontent.

"What, Cheryl? I brought him here so he can sign up for their housing and rehab programs," John said. "Seeing Yvonne is just an added perk."

Ruthie was too busy looking for Monroe to notice their regular sibling banter. It was the moment of truth. The real truth. There he was, standing by Mr. Pratt and looking as nervous as Ruthie felt.

"There he is, Cheryl," Ruthie said, instinctively grabbing her hand. "Let's walk over and meet him."

"Hi, Monroe."

"Hi, Ruthie. It's good to see you again."

"I have someone I want you to meet," Ruthie said, turning to Cheryl. "Cherylie-Bean, this is Monroe Jackson, your father. Monroe, this is Cheryl."

Tears immediately welled up in his eyes.

"I've waited so long to see you. So long."

Cheryl stood frozen in time, each second flooding particles of her being back into her body.

"May I hug you?"

"Um . . . yes."

Monroe's grip was the missing link to Cheryl's existence. On contact she felt whole, wanted, valued, loved. Tears of joy flowed from her core. He held her tight, like nothing and no one would ever harm her again. Her internal battle was complete. Their bond was instant, their embrace infectious. Ruthie held them both and wept aloud. Finally, a hardened piece of her soul was alive and at rest. Yvonne, Sheila, and John couldn't help but latch onto the new circle of love—gleaming from the radiant embrace of a father.

U S

Made in the USA
Monee, IL
30 August 2020